RIDE MY BEARD

HOT-BITES NOVELLA

JORDAN MARIE

JENIKA SNOW

RIDE MY BEARD

By Jordan Marie and Jenika Snow

www.JordanMarieRomance.com

support@jordanmarieromance.com

www.JenikaSnow.com

Jenika_Snow@yahoo.com

Copyright © September 2017 by Jordan Marie and Jenika Snow

First E-book Publication: September 2017

Photographer: Wander Aguiar

Cover model: Victorio Piva

Photo provided by: Wander Book Club

Cover Design: Letitia Hasser

Editor: Kasi Alexander

Lola

My entire life I have been in love with one man.

Ryker Stone.

It doesn't matter that he is more than double my age.

I don't care about the whispers that say he's too wild to ever be tamed.

I like that he's reckless.

He makes me feel like I can be uninhibited.

Truth is I saved myself for him.

I belong to him.

Ryker

I've had my eye on Lola for more years than I should admit.

Her beauty drew me in, but it was her innocence that trapped me.

I shouldn't want to claim her, but she's all I desire. So I stay close and make damn sure no one else touches her.

I'm all wrong for her, but too damn stupid and hard up to stay away.

She can run, but I'll follow.

By the time it's all said and done she'll be riding my beard.

Warning: This is a short and over-the-top dirty novella that will have you searching out your very own dirty mechanic. It's to the point and leaves nothing to the imagination, but then again, doesn't everyone like it that way? *wink*

HOT-BITES
NOVELLAS

Bought and Paid For
Ride My Beard

Where to find the authors:

Facebook
Newsletter
Pinterest
Twitter
Goodreads
Website

Facebook
Newsletter
Instagram

Twitter
Webpage
Goodreads

CHAPTER 1

Lola

$\mathscr{I}$ grab two beers and set them on my tray, turn, and walk toward the table, moving around horny, drunken guys as they try to grab my ass. But this is the norm at the bar where I work.

The Bottom of the Barrel, which name is pretty accurate for the customers who show up here, is busy as usual. If I didn't need the money, and wasn't always guaranteed a handful of tips at the end of the night—mainly because the guys think I'm sleazy and roll that way—I'd walk away from this place and never look back.

But as it is, the shitty town I live in doesn't have very many options of employment, especially for an eighteen-year-old with a family that has made sure everyone views her as trailer-park trash.

A mother who has a steady number of random men

rolling between her sheets and a father who only sees me as a one-night-stand mistake. This is the life that has always been my constant.

The music is loud, the jukebox in the corner older than I am. It's got buttons missing and a few songs skip constantly. But for the crowd that comes into the bar it's good enough.

The only thing they care about is slinging back cheap drinks, getting lap dances from the loose women who hang around town, and asking me for fifty-dollar blowjobs after my shift like I'll finally give in and do it one of these nights.

I take another order and go back to the bar, waiting until Slim makes his way toward me.

"A Jack and Coke and two Millers."

He doesn't say anything as he fills the order, but it's busy as hell tonight and we're both running on steam. My feet ache, and my shorts are a bit too small, but then again it's what gets me those killer tips.

I might dress so I show off a bit of skin, but I'm not easy. And if any of these assholes knew I was a virgin, that I've never even been felt up because I chose that, because I wanted it as a consenting adult, they would probably become even more disgusting than they already are.

I turn and look at the bar, the crowd thick, the air hot and heavy. This place is such a dump, with half the customers missing teeth, their guts hanging over their too-big belt buckles, and the stains on their shirts as prominent as the watermarks that line the ceiling.

I'm about to turn around and grab the orders that Slim put on my tray when I notice the front door swing open. Despite how hot I am, the beads of sweat between my breasts trickling down, I freeze. Chills race along my spine, move over my arms, and I swear it's as if this icy touch has a hold on me.

There, walking in like he owns the damn place—which holy hell, does he ever—is Ryker Stone.

His pants have that worn appearance, and God, does he look good in them. The silver chain that hangs from his pocket and down across his thigh catches the light briefly. He's wearing a t-shirt, that, although it fits him perfectly, also tells of the power he wields.

He's not a huge guy, not muscular like a bodybuilder. But he is tall, toned, ripped in every aspect of the word. He's lean with cuts of muscle that tell a person he'll kick their ass and not have any trouble doing it.

My throat is so dry, my tongue suddenly feeling too thick. He's older than me, by a couple decades, in fact. But I don't care about any of that.

I have wanted him since I was sixteen years old and saw him working under the hood of a car. Grease had covered him in the best of ways. And his hands—God, his hands—are so big, with veins that are roped up his muscular forearms. Every time I see them my legs get weak, I grow wet between my legs, and my breathing becomes ragged as I think of all the things he could do to me with those hands. I might be a virgin, but it's purely by choice. I'm not shy about the things I want… It's just I want those things with Ryker Stone. He makes me think filthy thoughts.

I look into his face and take in his beard, one I image pressed between my thighs as he eats me out…

"Order up," Slim shouts over the music so I can hear.

5

I force myself to turn around, grab the tray, and deliver the drinks. But even though I'm not looking at Ryker I can feel his gaze on me. I swear it's like he's taking my clothes off, just tearing the material from my body so he can get to the good parts.

And God, do I want him to get to the good parts.

CHAPTER 2

Ryker

I feel her gaze on me the minute I walk into the bar, and my dick hardens slowly against the inside of my thigh. I go to my usual table in the corner. I hate this fucking bar. There's nothing here to like, except for one thing. Lola Webb.

She's the only reason I've been coming here for over a year. I don't touch her. She's not mine. She's too fucking young and the kind of woman a man could lose his head over. So I stay away, as much as I can.

Still, I'm so fucking pussy-whipped that I've been coming to this bar, eating their shitty food, and drinking their watered-down beers for a year, not because I want to be here, but because I know I'll see her. Up until six months ago she only worked in the kitchen—because she wasn't old enough to serve alcohol. I hate that she slings drinks to the assholes here, but I'm not claiming her, and the she-bitch-cunt-from-hell she calls a mother sure doesn't support her. So, Lola's always earned her own way. I admire that, even if I don't like the way she does it.

Lola has a spirit about her that I like. She's free, self-sufficient and she refuses to take shit off of anyone. It's the kind of spirit a man—a real man—nurtures. Fuck. The truth is, I like everything about the little spitfire. *Every. Fucking. Thing* —*save one.*

I've forced myself to stay away from her because of her age. Even now she's barely legal at just eighteen. She's much too innocent for a hardened, filthy asshole like me to touch and she deserves a hell of a lot better than an old, broken-down grease monkey. So I stay here, watching her. Sitting just one table over from the tables that she takes care of. All that is on purpose.

If I had my fucking way I'd throw her over my shoulder, take her back to my place, and she would never leave. I'd probably tie her to my fucking bed.

An image of Lola bound to my bed and completely naked springs to my mind. My dick jerks at the image. She'd have to depend on me for everything. I'd be the one to feed her, bathe her...brush her hair. She would be completely at my mercy—forced to ask me for whatever she wanted or needed. *Maybe even beg.*

I could have groaned at that image, and the filthy fucking thoughts slamming into my head.

The idea alone is so potent it goes to my head like a fucking drug. One of the nameless waitresses brings my usual bottle of bourbon over and a glass. She tries to make small talk, but I ignore her. I'm only here for one reason and it's not her.

My gaze is glued to Lola's ass, round, tight, and fucking delicious, molded against those denim cut-off shorts she definitely had to be poured into. I throw back my first drink, so pissed my hand literally shakes. Her fucking ass cheeks are hanging out of the back of her shorts. I can literally see the curve that leads to the promise land—which means every fucker in here can see it too.

The view gets even better when she turns around. The tight black tank she wears hugs those tits of hers like a second skin. Every time she takes a step they sway and do this seductive dance that draws a man's eyes. There's no fucking way she's wearing a bra. My heart rate speeds and my fucking breathing goes ragged as I wonder if I could see her damn nipples if she were closer. I bet I could and I bet they'd be small and get so fucking hard for me. The kind of nipples a man could wrap his tongue around and suck hard, turning them bright red before biting into them and letting the thrill of pain explode over her body.

I force myself to take another drink and count backwards from fifty. I remind myself of all the reasons I shouldn't touch Lola Webb. I do all this while my body is reminding me that I haven't fucked a woman in over a year, because the only woman my dick seems to want is the one woman I'm trying to deny myself.

Fucking hell...

CHAPTER 3

Lola

*W*hy I thought tonight would be any different I don't know. Ryker spends the entire evening nursing a bottle of bourbon, staring at me but doing nothing. It's enough to drive a girl insane.

"Damn it, Lo, watch where you're going!" Tina, the other waitress working with me, yells. I look up just in time to avoid crashing into her.

"Sorry, Tina. I was…distracted."

"You were eye-fucking Mr. Hot, broody, and a whole lot of trouble over there," she mutters. I'd try to deny it, but there's not much I can say.

"I should just give up," I whine, feeling completely out of my comfort zone and frustrated. The man sets my body on fire just with a look. I can tell he wants me. *Why won't he do anything about it?*

"You should, but only because he's too damn old for you,"

Tina answers. "You need to leave men like Ryker to women like me. He'd scare you to death. Cut your teeth on boys your age before you try to wrangle a man like that between your sheets. Fuck, Ryker would probably have you running away the moment he whipped his cock out."

I have to literally pull myself back from snarling at her.

If she knew how in love with Ryker I was, she'd think I was insane. Hell, maybe I am. I've loved that man since I was sixteen and I've been praying and praying he'd notice me. I can still remember the day. I had just turned sixteen and my mother's shitty car needed some repair work. She pulled it into Ryker's garage and got him to fix her brakes. She tried to pay him for fixing her car—and in Mom's world that didn't include money. I can still remember how stunned I was when he turned her down.

"I didn't fix the fucking brakes for you. Your girl should be safe and have someone looking out for her," he shrugged, ignoring her. But his dark, almost black eyes stared straight at me. It felt as if his gaze was marking me, branding me from the inside.

Until that moment no one had really given a shit about me. My life consisted of finding a job and working all the hours I could, trying to finish school, and trying to stay out of the reach of the horny losers Etta Mae—my mother —brought home.

"What do you mean, *'scare me to death'?*" I ask Tina, shaking my memories of the past away.

"Word on the street is that man is a freak in the bedroom and packs a huge cock."

I didn't even comment on the dick part. "A freak how?"

"See? That right there is proof you're not made for a man like him. The talk is he's into public sex, whips and ropes, and any of the other kinky shit a man can get in his head," she says.

I feel my eyes go round as I imagine what Tina just said. I immediately get a picture of Ryker taking control of my body. I look out across the crowd. My gaze zeros in on his table. He's staring right at me—*that can't be my imagination.*

I picture myself walking over to him and taking my clothes off, demanding he take me right there with everyone watching us. I'd never do it, but the fantasy of it makes me flush all over with a heat I can't explain. I can feel the insides of my thighs coat in my excitement. *What would he do? Would he fuck me right here in front of everyone? Would he finally claim me in all the ways I've dreamed of over the years?*

"Oh," I whisper lamely, my body so excited that getting through the rest of my shift may be a problem.

"Get him out of your mind, little girl. You're in over your head." She snorts and then laughs, leaving me to feel like an idiot.

If only it were that simple.

CHAPTER 4

Ryker

I must have been sitting here for hours, just watching Lola, envisioning all the dirty fucking things I want to do to her. I've been milking the bourbon, and with the bottle half empty I have a good buzz going on. I know I should leave before I do something I might regret.

As it is, I am harder than fucking steel, my cock pressed against the zipper of my jeans, wanting to be out and buried deep inside Lola's tight pussy. I bet she will be hot, and so damn pink. I bet she's a virgin too.

Fuck.

Just thinking that she never had a man between her thighs, that she still has her cherry intact, has me gripping the edge of the table so hard I won't be surprised if the wood cracks.

I watch Lola come out of the back room, a couple of fresh

bottles of Jack in her grasp. She bends over to put the bottles on the lower shelf and her jean shorts rise up. Damn, just a small piece of denim covering the sweet spot I want to bury my face in.

But because I don't want to be a dirty bastard I toss a few bills on the table and leave. I need some fresh air, maybe even a smoke to calm this raging arousal rushing through me. I pull out a cigarette and place it between my lips. I grab the lighter and light the end before inhaling deeply. I need to quit this shit, but the nicotine hits right to the problem areas and soothes the shit out of it.

The bar door swings open and a couple of rowdy guys stumble out. It is clear they are drunk by the way they slur their words, but I ignore them. I have other things on my mind, things that include getting Lola naked in my bed, screaming my name as she comes.

You dirty fucking bastard.

I stay out here for half an hour or more, trying to resist the urge to go back inside. I know the minute I do, my dick will come alive at the mere sight of Lola. The damn thing is still semi hard, but manageable, less noticeable.

It's a mistake, but I just need one more look at her before I go home and jack off to my hand. I snub out my cigarette, about to head back inside, when I hear the shattering of bottles.

Maybe I should have minded my own damn business, but I find myself walking around the corner and stepping into the alley. One of the parking lot lights is on, the muted yellow glow casting shadows over the twin dumpsters.

At first I can't make out what is going on. I can only see

the two drunks I noticed earlier standing by the dumpsters. But then I see her small form between them, the trash bag she clearly had been taking outside now sitting by her feet. I don't know what in the hell is going on, but the two assholes are crowding her. It has this rage burning brightly inside of me. I find myself stalking closer to them, my hands curled into tight fists at my side, my focus solely on the two pricks who will soon be on the asphalt.

And then I hear the foul, disgusting things that they are saying to Lola. I growl low and reach one of the guys, gripping the nape of his neck and yanking him backward. He falls to his ass on the ground, and I immediately go for his buddy.

I have the front of his shirt twisted in my hold, and lift him easily off the ground. I toss him away and hear his body slam into the brick wall. I face both of the pricks then and watch as they pick their sorry asses up off the ground. Maybe it's the anger coming off of me in violent waves, or maybe they're not as stupid as I think, but they both hightail it out of there.

I turn to face Lola and see her staring at me wide-eyed. I want to take her in my arms and just hold her in that moment, let her know that everything will be okay, that I'll never let anyone hurt her. And because I have all these insane emotions running through me, I do just that.

I pull her in close, her small body forming perfectly to mine. She smells good, like sweet vanilla, and that makes me even more intoxicated. I cup the back of her head but she pulls back slightly and looks up at me. Because I'm a dumb motherfucker I know what I want to do in that moment.

I want to kiss her.
I want to fuck her.
I want to make her know she's mine.

CHAPTER 5

Lola

*H*e's going to kiss me. He's going to kiss me.

The thought repeats in my mind over and over. I run the tip of my tongue over my lips and fight down my nerves. My heart is thundering in my chest like a herd of wild elephants. Ryker has to be able to hear it. I stand up on my tiptoes, leaning into him, begging him silently to kiss me.

I inhale deeply, and the air I suck in is thick with the very essence of him. Sandalwood, old leather and a tinge of motor oil are scents that I always associate with Ryker. Some women might curl their nose at it, but not me. It makes me feel…alive.

His hands are at the small of my back and I feel his fingers just barely brushing the hem of my shirt. They are rough from hours of working on cars. The harshness of them tickles against my sensitive skin and sends a wave of goosebumps up my spine and on the back of my neck. My entire body has excitement running through it that leaves me breathless.

I put my hands on his chest, my knees suddenly weak. He lets out a low rumble that I first feel vibrate under my hands and then hear from his gruff voice.

"You shouldn't be out here by yourself," he says and takes a step from me, his hands moving to my hips as he roughly pushes me away. He keeps his hands on me until I steady myself. I immediately miss the warmth of his body, his masculine scent and the feeling of being safe in his arms. I mourn the loss of him silently for a moment while I gather my thoughts.

"I was only doing my job," I defend quietly, wondering what he would do if I ran my fingers through his long hair and pushed it off of his face.

"You nearly got yourself raped," he says, his lips almost curling in distaste and I hate that he is looking at me like that.

"I didn't, though. You saved me," I tell him, trying to hold onto my pride.

"Only by chance. Another five minutes and I wouldn't have been here. If you're going to hold down a job like this, little girl, you can't be stupid," he growls at me again and his condescending words and tone spur my anger.

"I'm fine," I mumble, feeling foolish for thinking he was planning on kissing me. Clearly he wasn't. *I was delusional.*

"You need a fucking keeper," he growls, raking his hands through his hair in frustration.

"Well, I don't have one. I never have and unless you're planning on taking the job, I better get back to work," I huff.

I go to step around him so I can go back inside the bar. I

take about three steps before he reaches out and grabs my arm, pulling me close to him.

"I don't know what kind of boys you are used to, but you need to take care how you talk to a man, little one," he warns, his voice dropping down into a deep timbre that sends shivers of awareness all through me.

"Ryker—"

"Before one teaches you exactly what to do with that mouth," he interrupts, his voice almost a growl. His thumb traces over the bottom of my lip. I can't stop myself from opening my mouth enough so that the tip of his thumb is right there. I'm dying to suck that digit into my mouth. *What would he do?*

Instead, I let the tip of my tongue lick against it, tasting his skin. We're standing so close that I can imagine it, and the deep hue in his eyes seems to deepen in color. I could get lost in the inky black depths. His pupils dilate, and I might be a novice but I can hear the change in his breathing. He's excited. *I'm exciting him.*

"Are you volunteering for the job?" I ask him, my heart pounding, my voice sounding as breathless as I feel.

He stares at me a moment. Mentally I'm screaming at him to say yes, to do something, anything to relieve this ache inside of me. For a moment I really think he's going to. I envision him pushing me up against the side of the building and fucking me raw. My legs tremble from the very thought of it. And then...

"You don't know what you're inviting. Run back inside before you get yourself into trouble, Lola. You're not ready for what I would do to you."

His words make me ache; they make my heart clench

19

painfully. I want to argue with him. I almost do, because I can see the interest in his eyes and I see the hard outline of his dick against his jeans. I'm close to asking him to show me what he'd do—begging him to make me his. Then Tina's words come back to me and I feel fear.

What if she's right? What if he's right? I'm a virgin. I might know what a man and woman do with each other, I might even dream of doing that with Ryker, but when it came down to it, would I panic? Would I disappoint him? What if I wasn't enough for him?

"Lola, you okay out here?" my boss yells from the door, interrupting us. My gaze stays locked on Ryker.

"Yeah, I'm fine. The damn trash bag ripped open." I lie easily, not wanting to admit what just happened.

"Leave it. I'll have one of the guys pick it up. Get back in here where you're safe. I don't like you being out here alone too long."

"You better go," Ryker says, and I nod my head in agreement. Disappointment curls in my stomach and I think I see it flashing in Ryker's eyes too.

"Maybe if you explained what you expected from me first, I wouldn't be scared at all, Ryker. I really don't think I would be—but only if it was you," I whisper, feeling a little out of my depth. Handling drunks and warding off men is one thing. Admitting to the one man I've always loved that I want him—even if I am clueless—is quite another.

I walk back to the bar and step inside, carefully closing the door. My mind is too consumed with doubts and fears. It makes it hard to breathe. I don't look at Ryker. I'm afraid of what I'll see on his face. Or worse, what he would say about my admission.

I hope I see him tomorrow. I hope I didn't push him away forever. I don't think I could handle it if I did. I need him to be here in the bar tomorrow. I need him to talk to me. Because the only thing I'm sure of in my whole, messed-up life is that I want Ryker Stone to be the man to take my virginity. I want him to be my first, to show me everything he knows about sex, because I'm tired of being a virgin.

And maybe, just maybe if I learn enough to please him, he might want me back. If I please him, maybe he'll keep me. Because Ryker Stone is the only man I want to touch me...*ever.*

CHAPTER 6

Ryker

I toss my keys on the table and go to the fridge to grab a beer. Truth is, I don't need more alcohol, but after the interaction I had with Lola earlier tonight, I need something to take the edge off.

I pop the cap and drink half the beer before setting it on the counter and exhaling. My dick is hard, and the blood rushes through my body. I want to go back to the bar and take Lola right then and there, just press her to the fucking dumpster, push down her shorts and panties, and push my hard dick into her sweet pussy.

I moan at the thought.

I have no doubt she'll be tight as hell, sucking at my cock, milking the cum from me. I groan at the thoughts that slam into my head, the images that are so filthy I could get off right in my jeans. I am a dirty bastard, and I make no claims that I'm not.

Lola deserves sweet and gentle, a man who will worship her body in a delicate way. I am rough and hardened, and used to raw fucking sex.

All I can think about are those assholes trying to touch her, trying to have her. She is mine. I know that with everything in me. I tried to warn her off tonight, even though I know that trying to pretend I can walk away and let her be with some other prick is unrealistic. I've known that I wanted her since it was legal, since I allowed myself to see her as a woman.

I was trying to give her a choice. I really was. I wasn't prepared for her soft voice to pull me in further. I can still hear her words ringing in my ears.

"Maybe if you explained what you expected from me first, I wouldn't be scared at all, Ryker. I really don't think I would be— but only if it was you."

How can a man fight that? I can't. It doesn't matter that the things I want to do to her are fucking dirty, maybe even depraved. She as much as offered herself to me and I can't walk away. It's not possible. No other woman could take her place, because it's not just about having my cock buried deep in her pussy. It's not just about filling her up with my cum and marking her as mine. It's also about keeping her close. It's about keeping her safe. I can do that better than any other man alive. I was born to do that. *She's mine.*

I know the shitty life she's had, that her mom is a whore who doesn't even care about her. I know that she's all alone, just trying to make a place for herself, just trying to survive.

I'm older than her, more experienced, and I can show her what she needs, what she's never had.

I can show Lola that she doesn't have to be alone. I'll fuck up anyone who tries to hurt her, who tries to stand in my way from claiming her as mine. Even if the best thing for her is for me to walk away, for me to not get involved, that's a dead end.

Going to the bar every night has proven that over and over again.

No, I know what I want and that's Lola as mine, and I won't try and fucking hide it or deny it any longer.

She invited me into her life; now it's time to claim her. *No more waiting.*

I go into the bathroom and crank the shower, making sure the temperature is cold enough that it might get my arousal under control.

I strip out of my clothing and climb in, the initial shock of the frigid droplets on my flesh dimming the hunger that consumes me. My dick is rock hard, my need for her going strong.

Because I am done fighting Lola's pull. I give in.

I reach down and grab my cock, stroking myself from root to tip. My forearm flexes, and I place my other hand on the tile in front of me. Hanging my head, I close my eyes and really start to work my palm over my shaft, faster and harder, thinking only of Lola.

I squeeze my eyes tight, picturing Lola on my bed, her legs spread, her pink virgin pussy on display. I imagine myself between her thighs, my mouth right by her sweet cunt, my warm breath bathing her pussy lips. I'd devour her, lick and suck her until she screamed my name, until she begged me to stop...pleaded for more, and her sweet pussy dripped on my beard.

My balls draw up tight to my body, my breathing

becoming ragged. I'm going to come so fucking hard and it's all from thinking about Lola.

Fuck, I want her so damn badly, even if I know that it is wrong, even if I know she deserves better. And as much as I should stay away, give her space, let her find someone who will be gentle with her, I know I can't.

I won't.

I can't walk away from her. I can't let some other fucker touch her. She's mine, and nothing will ever change that. No one will take her from me.

I come then, my seed spraying out of my cock and landing on the tile before me. I groan and grit my teeth, letting the pleasure wash over me, letting it consume me.

I want to make Lola feel good, have her wrapped up in everything that is me. I want her smelling like me, feeling my body.

I want my cock in her pussy. I want my seed filling up her womb.

What I need is Lola as my woman, my wife...the mother of my children.

When I'm drained dry I let go of my dick and place both hands on the tiled wall. I breathe harshly, my eyes still closed, my thoughts still on Lola. No, I am not going to walk away from her.

I am going to make her mine.

CHAPTER 7

Lola

"Order up, Lola!" Slim yells and I do my best to give him a smile. The truth is I don't feel like smiling. My head hurts, my feet ache, my back is tight—and that's just the beginning of my ailments. My chief complaint is that I'm almost through my entire shift and Ryker hasn't shown up. He's always here. *Always.*

I feel so stupid. *Why did I have to sound so pathetic? Why couldn't I have just played it cool?* If Tina had been in my shoes she would have just attacked Ryker and been in his bed that night. I had to act like a stupid, terrified virgin. *How do I ever expect someone like Ryker Stone to take me serious if I can't even act like an adult around him?*

I put the round of beers a group of customers ordered down on the table. I'll be glad when these idiots go home. There are four of them here for a bachelor party. Hell, they were shitfaced when they got here, and their comments are getting more lewd with each round. I'm doing my best to avoid the grabbing hands. One of the men thinks to get smart and trips me. Because of these damn heels I wear, I can't keep my balance and fall straight into the lap of the loudest drunk of them all. He's also the one that is supposed to be getting married.

He latches a hand painfully onto my breast. I cry out in shock and hurt. I'm trying to calm my panic, getting ready to bring my serving tray back against the man's face when suddenly the hand is gone.

"You think you can touch what's mine?" Ryker growls in a voice so cold and so deadly it feels like everyone and everything in the bar comes to a complete standstill.

"Hey, man, we're just trying to have a little fun. Dressed like she is, she's asking for it. Don't worry, we'll treat her good," the idiot says, obviously not seeing how dangerous the situation is. Everyone else can sense the violence coming from Ryker, including his friends, because they've gone quiet.

"Lola, get up," Ryker commands—and it is most definitely a command. Until that moment, I was so intent on watching Ryker that I didn't realize I was still sitting in the man's lap. I quickly get up, nervously moving aside.

"Ryker—" I start, but one look from him stops the rest of the words in my throat. He's pissed. He was mad last night, but that pales in comparison to the fury coming off of him right now.

"Slim," he calls out.

"Yeah, man?"

"Unlock your office," he says, but his gaze is glued to the man who grabbed my breast. He's still holding the asshole's

27

hand and it's an intense grip. It's the type of hold that I know will leave a bruise. Maybe the guy is starting to sober up too, because he's not trying to fight with Ryker, or even get away from him. He's barely breathing—almost as if he's afraid resisting too much will unleash the anger Ryker is carrying. The man is obviously smarter than I gave him credit for.

"Buddy, listen. We don't want any problem. I didn't know she was yours. No harm, no foul here. What do you say?"

"Lola, go to Slim's office and wait for me," he says and his voice drops down. It's much quieter now, almost deadly.

"Ryk—"

"I'm barely hanging on right now, Lola. Do it and do not argue," he all but growls out.

I should be terrified. The anger and force behind Ryker's words should chill me. The look in his eyes as he's staring down at the drunken asshole who hurt me should make me run away. Instead, I'm excited. I won't lie; I'm nervous as hell. But Ryker Stone just called me his in front of everyone in the bar. *His.*

"Okay, Ryker," I say softly, touching his shoulder as I walk around him. He takes his gaze away from the other man— just briefly.

"When I get back there, Lola, you better have your ass bared and bent over the table."

"What? Ryker, I..." I cannot believe he is saying these things, let alone in front of everyone.

"I told you to protect yourself and to be careful. You weren't. It's time you find out what happens when you jeopardize what's mine."

"Now, listen here. I know—"

"You offered yourself to me last night, do you remember, Lola?" he prompts.

God, I should be humiliated he's saying these things, but the truth is I'm excited, aroused.

"Jesus. You're all fucking crazy," the drunk slurs out. He's jerking his hand away now, but it's useless. Ryker's not about to let him go. All he manages to accomplish is making Ryker angrier. Ryker shifts and maneuvers so the man is now standing up. Ryker spins him around so he's facing him, then drives his elbow into the man's side, causing him to bend in half, crying out in pain.

"Lola?" Ryker prompts again.

"I remember." I swallow, wondering now if it is nerves or excitement making me feel more than a little dizzy.

"You told me to tell you what I wanted first. So I'm telling you. When I get back there you better be in the position I want you, the way I want you, and ready for your punishment. Do you understand?"

"Ye...yes," I stutter, wondering why my nipples pebble at his instructions. I can feel how wet I am now, my panties soaked clean through. His crass words and demanding tone should turn me off, but it doesn't. At the very least, I should be embarrassed that the entire bar is listening and knows what Ryker will be doing to me soon.

I'm not—not really.

I hold my head up all the way to the back of the building where the office is. Out of the corner of my eye I see Tina and I know she's looking at me with envy. I can't resist smiling.

CHAPTER 8

Ryker

I have the fucker's shirt wrapped tightly around my fist as I haul him out of the bar. When we are outside, I toss him away from me and he lands on his ass in the parking lot. He looks up at me, maybe wanting to retaliate, maybe thinking he can go up against me.

I want him to try because right now I am feeling pretty pissed. He put his hands on what is mine and I want the fucker to pay for it.

He picks himself up off the ground and we stare at each other for a few seconds. "Come on, motherfucker, come after me and let me beat your ass."

I can hear the door to the bar opening behind me, and have to assume his friends have come out. Maybe they're smarter than him and will take his ass home.

Finally he just shakes his head and runs a hand across his face. His friends move around me and it's clear they are smarter than I've given them credit for. They walk away from me and head to their car, but I still feel pretty pissed off.

I run my hand across my jaw and exhale roughly. Part of me is angry at Lola, mainly because I hate that she's in this situation constantly. I don't want her working at this bar, don't want bastards looking at her, touching her...thinking they have a chance with her.

I turn and look at the bar, knowing she's waiting for me in the back room. I curl my hands into tight fists at my sides and grin. What I'm about to show her, do to her, will make it abundantly clear that she is mine.

I ignore everybody and everything as I head back into the bar, toward Slim's office. I don't bother knocking before I swing the door open. I stare at her, her body so much smaller than mine, so innocent and vulnerable...so feminine.

My arousal is strong, like this fucking beast inside of me. I kick the door shut behind me with my foot and reach around to lock it. No one is going to interrupt this.

I could ease her into things, give her some sweet-talking and be gentle. But I know she wants me the same way I want her, and going slow is more than I can offer her right now.

"Take off those tiny as fuck shorts, pull your panties down, turn around and bend over the desk," I order her, leaving no room for argument—heaven help her if she tries.

She hesitates for just a moment, but then I lower my gaze and watch as she unbuttons her shorts and pulls the zipper down. My heart starts thundering then, and I feel my cock jerk violently. The fucker gets hard in that instant, pressing against the fly of my jeans and demanding freedom.

When her shorts and panties are pushed down to her

ankles, I can't help but growl at the sight of the trimmed thatch of hair that covers her pussy. She turns around and bends over like a good girl. With her back toward me now, her ass in the air, I reach down and palm my dick through my jeans. I groan at the pleasure that shoots up my spine.

I walk over to Lola and don't stop myself from reaching out and cupping one smooth, peach-colored cheek. I want to smack the flesh, spank her good and hard until my handprint is covering her pale flesh.

"Baby, I'm about to show you that working here, being around these motherfuckers, has consequences." She looks over her shoulder at me, her eyes wide, her mouth parted.

"But it's not my fault there are a bunch of assholes who come here," she defends and if I wasn't so fucking hard and ready to go off, I would smile.

No, it wasn't her fault, but I need an excuse to touch her in the way I want to, in the way I need to. I also need her to understand that when it comes to her, to her safety—fuck, anything to do with her, I'm not about to be reasonable.

"Tell me you want my hands on you, want me to smack this perfect ass until the pleasure and pain melt into one, until my mark is on your body and you know that you're mine."

She still looks at me over her shoulder, her eyes so wide, her pretty, pink lips still parted.

"Tell me, dammit." My voice is harsh, rough, exactly how I'm going to be with her. I won't be satisfied until she is screaming out for more.

"Yes," she says softly and I can hear the need in her voice. Her hands are stretched out in front of her, her fingers curled around the edge of the desk.

I take a step back and put my foot between her legs to kick her feet apart. I look down at her ass, her legs spread wide enough that I can see her pussy lips. They are pink and glossy, and slightly swollen from her arousal. My mouth waters and my balls draw up tight to my body.

I want to reach down and unzip my jeans, pull my dick out, and align it right at the entrance of her pussy hole. I want to shove it deep inside of her, claiming her cherry and making her know she's mine.

But instead of doing that, I bring my hand back and strike her ass. The spanking I deliver is hard enough that my palm stings, and I see her back bow. I know that the pain is there. I do this over and over again, bringing my palm down on the fleshy globes, seeing the skin shake from my actions. I'm careful never to land my hand in the same spot twice. This is about teaching her to need what only I can give her. I'm not going to physically hurt her; she's precious to me. I merely need to teach her that there is pleasure in the pain.

Her ass is a beautiful shade of red, and I can hear her panting, hear the sweet moans of hunger as they leave her mouth. I know it hurts, but I also know it feels good. It's several long minutes before I finally stop spanking her and take a step back. I'm breathing hard, my dick like a steel rod between my legs, and sweat dotting my brow.

Before I can even think about what I'm doing, before I even know what I'm doing, I'm on my knees behind her. My hands are on her ass cheeks, spreading them wide, taking in the pretty pink cunt that I have revealed.

She's so fucking wet for me. Her juices are covering her inner thighs and her clit is engorged and peeking out for my mouth. I lean in and run my tongue from her clit to her pussy hole, lapping up her cream, swallowing the musky sweetness that she produces for me.

Only for me.

Her legs are shaking and I push my way between them, using my shoulders to make sure her thighs are spread good and wide for me. I devour her then, licking and sucking the lips of her pussy, taking her clit into my mouth and drawing circles around it with my tongue.

She's moaning loudly for me now, and I renew my efforts. I dig my fingers into her ass cheeks, holding her in place as I eat her out. But all too soon I pull away, stand up, and help her up off the table. I turn around and she looks up at me with this dazed, almost crazed expression. But I'm not nearly done with her yet.

I walk over to the chair behind the desk and take a seat, wrap my hands around her waist, and lift her up so she is now sitting in front of me.

"Put your feet on the arms of the chair," I demand as I look into her eyes.

When she's in the position I want her in I look at her cunt spread open for me. She's so fucking ready for me, so primed for my cock. But tonight I'm not going to fuck her. There are things I need to discuss with Lola before I take that pretty cherry as my own.

I reach around and grab her ass, pulling her forward so her bottom is right on the edge of the desk. And then I start devouring her again. I lick and suck, working my way through every part of her pussy until her stomach is heaving up and down and she's begging me for more.

And just when I have gotten started, Lola starts rocking her hips back and forth. She has her arms behind her,

34

bracing herself so she can find more pleasure. She grinds her pussy on my mouth, all over my beard, crying out as she gets closer to exploding. I sit there and let her do her thing, let her ride me until she's crying out and coming all over my mouth.

I lap at the juices that come from her. I use my thumbs to pull her pussy lips apart and lick at every single inch of her. I twirl my tongue around her clit until she's begging me to stop, pleading that she's too sensitive. Only then do I pull away, her cream all over my mouth and beard, her satisfaction filling me.

"You're mine." The words come from me on their own, demanding, and set in stone. Her mouth is open and she's breathing hard, her chest rising and falling, her tits pressed up and out, her nipples rock hard.

"I'm yours."

Yeah, she fucking is.

CHAPTER 9

Lola

"*L*ook at me, Lola," Ryker commands.

I'm standing awkwardly by the door—now fully dressed, my head down, and trying to process what just happened. It's everything I've been dreaming about—maybe more, but now that it's over I'm unsure about what comes next, how I'm supposed to act. I don't know what Ryker expects of me. No, I know what he expects...*all of it. All of me.* Which leaves me standing here like a dummy, using all the courage I have just to raise my head and look Ryker in the eye.

The minute I do I see the ownership in his gaze. I see the satisfaction on his face. I also see signs of my arousal on his mustache and beard. I feel my face heat and I know I'm blushing. The harsh lines on Ryker's face soften and he comes closer, hooks his hand around my neck, and pulls me into his body. He's tall and made up of lean muscle, but he encircles me and I feel tiny and feminine next to him. I feel protected and safe. That's it exactly. It's a strange sensation, but I have to acknowledge it. Ryker makes me feel *safe.*

"You're mine." He repeats his earlier words and I can't stop the small smile that spreads on my face, because he sounds kind of like a caveman.

"I know," I acknowledge.

"Are you ashamed?" he asks, his voice all growly. His other hand comes up and he holds my head between them, as if he is preventing me from looking away. There's an emotion on his face I can't name, but it makes me feel like my answer has more weight than I can understand.

"No. Of course not," I murmur. Nothing could make me ashamed of what we just did. I feel like I've wanted it my whole life. There's still a part of me wondering if it's really happened. Maybe I've dreamed it for so long, this is just another fantasy and I'll wake up and none of it will have ever happened.

"Then why are you suddenly so shy, when minutes ago you were riding my face and begging for more?" His question makes me squirm a little from embarrassment, but more because I can feel a fresh wave of excitement roll through me, making me even wetter. My body instantly craves the relief I know only Ryker can give me. He's a forbidden fruit and now that I've had one taste, I just want more.

"Slim," I start, but then stop, unsure of how to explain it.

"Does he have a claim on you, Lola? Has he laid a hand on you?" Ryker growls, his hold growing stronger, losing its tenderness and becoming almost bruising with its force.

"No! I've never thought of any man like that except for

you, Ryker. It's just he... They all know what we did in here. It's...embarrassing."

"Nothing we do together will ever embarrass me. It should never embarrass you. You belong to me, Lola. You give your body to me when, how and where I say. Do you understand?" he asks, and his frank words should bother me, but they don't. They make my body flush with heat.

"Yes, Ryker," I answer, unable to say anything else. I'm hypnotized by the dark promises held in his gaze. My answer seems to please him because his hold gentles and he moves his thumb across my cheek.

"Good girl," he says and then, as if he's giving me praise, he kisses my forehead in the sweetest kiss I can ever remember feeling. "We'll come back to just how I want you, Lola, when it's time," he adds and looks positively sinful when he delivers that promise. It's a look that makes my knees weak. "Tell me exactly what you mean when you say you've never thought of giving yourself to anyone but me. Is that true?"

I swallow, nerves assaulting me, but I push through them. Now is not the time to get weak, not when I might be on the verge of having everything I've ever wanted.

"It is. I've always wanted my first to be you," I tell him, calling on courage that I didn't know I possessed.

"Your first? What exactly are you saying, Lola?" he questions, but he knows what I'm saying. The truth is there on his face and I read it plain as day. He wants me to tell him, though, and since I've come this far, I might as well jump in head first.

"I want... I've *always* wanted you to be the man who takes

my virginity, Ryker," I tell him and, though my face heats, I keep my gaze directly on him.

"I'm too old for you," he discounts, but I can tell he likes what I've said.

"Then you will know how to make it good for me," I tell him and then, because I can't stop myself, I bring my hand up to hold it against his. "You can make it good for both of us, teach me how to please you."

"You know what kind of man I am, Lola. You've heard the talk in town. I have needs a girl like you might not like," he growls, his body vibrating and I think it might be with desire.

Ryker Stone wants me.

"And I already told you, Ryker. If you took time to show me, nothing you would do to me would scare me."

"How do you know?" he asks, studying me closely and suddenly I know my entire future rests on how I answer this simple question.

"Because it's you and I'm yours. Ryker, I've always been yours. I've just been waiting for you to claim me," I tell him, my breath lodged in my chest as I wait to see how he answers my bold statement.

CHAPTER 10

Ryker

I know she is at the shop before I even see her. I swear I can smell her, can see the lines of her curves, taste the flavor of her pussy on my tongue. Hell, I've tasted her since we left that office and I held her close as we faced the bar. Everyone knew what we'd done, what I'd done to her.

Their focus had been on us, the surprise clear on their faces.

I didn't give a fuck. I pulled Lola closer, had my hand right on her luscious ass, and let every bastard know that she was mine.

"Someone's here to see you," Rocco calls out.

I roll out from under the car, my body covered in grease and sweat, my focus on the hot little ass in front of me. Lola stands there in these cutoff shorts, her long legs tanned, creamy, and so fucking smooth. I let my gaze travel up her thighs, over the small patch of denim that covers her delicious, sweet pussy, over her midriff that's shown, and up to her generous breasts.

Fuck, ever since I had my mouth on her cunt, felt her grinding her pussy on my lips, riding me like she was dying to get off, all I can think about is shoving my cock deep in her and tearing through her cherry.

I stand and grab a towel to wipe off the grease and sweat from my face. She's looking so fucking good I can't even think straight at the moment. All I can imagine is having my face buried between her thighs, eating her out until she comes all over my face. I want to do it over and over again, make her sore, sensitive because of my lips and tongue.

"Hey," she says softly, and glances down as if she's embarrassed.

I move closer to her, lift her head up with a finger under her chin, and lean in an inch. "Baby, those pink cheeks aren't necessary. I've had my mouth all over your virgin cunt, tasted your sweet arousal and claimed you as mine already." Her cheeks turn even redder.

I take her hand and lead her back to the office, shutting the door once we are inside. I can see that she's nervous, her pulse beating rapidly right below her ear. I want to run my tongue over it, feel how fast her heart is actually beating, taste her skin and memorize every part of her.

I wait for her to say something, tell me what she desires. I made myself perfectly clear the other night when I had my face between her thighs. Now it's up to Lola to make the next move.

She clears her throat and looks down at the ground, and I watch her cheeks become even pinker. I'm embarrassing her, but I like that. I like that she's on edge, that I make her feel this way.

I step closer and lift her chin up again with my finger, wanting to look in her eyes, wanting to let her know without actually saying anything that I'll give her whatever she wants.

She licks her lips, and I watch her tongue dart out and smooth over the pouty flesh. I want to see that mouth wrapped around my cock, her cheeks hollowed as her head moves up and down along the shaft.

"Tell me what you want, Lola. Tell me and it's yours."

She inhales slightly, and when she exhales, her warm, sweet breath moves along my neck. She looks up at me with this wide, innocent and vulnerable expression.

"I want what we did at the office. I want more of that, want to go further."

I watch as her pupils dilate, the darkness eating up the lighter color. I lean down close so our faces are at the same level. "Do you want me to take you back to my house, strip you naked, and touch every inch of your body?" She nods slowly, her breathing increasing. "Do you want me to spread those pretty thighs of yours, place my big fucking cock at your pussy hole, and push right through that cherry of yours?"

"Oh. God."

She closes her eyes and I move my hand behind her head, steadying her. I feel her relax against me, and pull her impossibly closer to me. Then I move my mouth to her ear and say softly, "I'm going to pick you up tonight, take you back to my house, and fuck you until you can't walk straight." I pull back, waiting for her to open her eyes and look at me.

There's some noise outside the office and she looks over to the side, the worry on her face clear.

"Or we can do it right here. I can push the shit off the table, bend you over, remove these little shorts of yours, and plunge my cock deep in your tight little body."

"You really don't care if anybody hears us, or what we are doing, do you?"

I shake my head slowly. "Lola, when it comes to you I want the whole fucking world to know that you're mine and what I do with you...*to* you." Then I lean in and kiss her harshly, plunging my tongue between her lips and making her see that my words are a promise. When I break away we are both breathing hard and heavy. "Tonight, Lola. Tonight you'll fully be mine."

CHAPTER 11

Lola

I look in the mirror for the hundredth time. I'm so nervous. Ryker called me and told me to dress up because he was taking me out tonight. I was excited and sad at the same time. I didn't envision us leaving the house. I had hoped...

It doesn't matter. If Ryker wants to take me out, then I'll be fine with that. I look at the black dress I'm wearing. It's not really fancy, but it does look flattering on me. It's loose and flowy, falling just below my knees. It has a V-neck that shows off just enough cleavage to be called sexy. It comes up on my arms but has these cut-out sleeves that expose my shoulders. My long hair is piled high on my head in this messy bun that somehow looks kind of classy.

Overall I think I look good, attractive and ready for tonight. But at the same time I don't know if it screams *'sexy, mature woman.'* Will Ryker be disappointed? I'm hoping having my hair up will make me appear older and worldlier —a woman fit to be on the arm of someone like Ryker Stone. I look at my choice of shoes. I should have just gone with the flats. After working all night the evening before, my feet hurt. Still, it's my first night off in forever and I'm going out with the man of my dreams—and hottest fantasies. I'm not about to do half-assed on this date.

With that in mind, I slip on the glossy black heels. I've nicknamed them fuck-me pumps. I've never worn them before, but then again, I've never wanted to be fucked by anyone other than Ryker. Now that this night is actually happening, I'm not taking any chances.

I just finish adjusting the strap on my heel when the knock sounds on my front door. I can almost feel my heart flip inside my chest as my tension cranks higher. I take a deep breath, trying to calm my nerves before I open the door. When I have a hold of the handle and pull it open, Ryker is standing there in his old, faded jeans. The denim fabric hugs his body like a second skin, lovingly clinging to his thighs and stretching in ways that make my knees weak. He's wearing a black t-shirt that looks soft and comfortable and I wonder how it would feel against my bare skin. I can feel wetness pool against my panties and coat the inside of my thighs. I have no idea how I'm supposed to go out with Ryker tonight when all I can think about is what he will do to me when we get back to his place.

His words play through my head, a promise of the dark, pleasurable things he'll do to me tonight.

I step back to let him inside, running my tongue against my lips because my mouth suddenly feels terribly dry.

"Hi," I murmur, my voice sounding deeper to my own

ears. Can he hear how much I want him? Somehow I think a man of Ryker's experience can.

"You look good enough to eat," he says, his hand reaching out to run a finger along the inside of my neck.

His words are dirty and we both know how he means them. Goosebumps pop up on my flesh and I have to bite my lip to keep from begging him to touch me in other places.

"You get all dressed up for me, Lola?" he asks, and I can't find my voice to answer. I nod my reply instead. Worry instantly assaults me when Ryker takes a step back, appraising me. "Turn around," his rough voice commands.

My gaze lifts up to his, startled. I don't think of disobeying him, however. I don't see how any woman could. I turn slowly, wondering if I will meet with his approval, or if he will be disappointed. Will he wish he had picked out someone older? Someone with more experience, someone who can please him in the way he wants? A woman who understands and anticipates all of his desires? I feel completely out of my depth. You would have thought after spending the time in the office where Ryker brought me to orgasm, I'd feel more at ease. It appears the opposite is true.

"Are you wearing anything under that dress, Lola?" he growls as I turn back to face him.

"My..." My words come to a stop when I begin to literally feel the vibration of Ryker's mood. At first I mistake it for anger, but one look at his face tells me that's not it. It's...*hunger*. "My panties," I whisper, suddenly feeling more secure.

"Take them off," he growls, issuing the order.

"I...I thought we were going out?" I question him.

"We are, but I want your pussy bare under that dress."

"Why?" I ask, and it's not that I'm that naïve, but I have this need to hear him tell me exactly why he wants me open to him.

"Because I'm going to fuck you with my fingers while we're at the restaurant," he tells me, crossing his arms at his chest as if daring me to deny him.

"What if... I mean... I might come..."

"Oh, you will definitely come, Lola," he agrees and this time his throaty voice sends shockwaves through me, and they all seem to center in my very wet pussy.

"People around us will hear me, Ryker. They will know."

"And every man there will be grabbing their cocks and wishing they were me. They'll all be wishing they could fuck your sweet little virgin cunt. But they won't, will they, Lola? They'll be nutting off in their hands instead. And do you know why, Lola?" he asks, his dark gaze almost burning me with its intensity.

"Because I belong to you," I tell him, instinctively knowing what he wants from me.

"Damn straight. Now I'm not telling you again. Take off those panties and hand them to me." I move to turn around to go down the hall, but Ryker stops me by reaching out and grabbing my arm. "Where are you going?"

"I was going to my room to take off—"

"You'll take them off right here in front of me," he interrupts. My breath shudders through my body and I feel my excitement slide from my pussy, soaking my panties and dripping along my thighs. I'm so wet it's embarrassing. I can even smell my own arousal. If I go out without panties on, others will too. They'll all know I'm dying to have Ryker's cock inside of me. They'll know and I realize that's exactly what he wants.

I reach under my dress, hooking my fingers in the waistband of the small black lace thong, thanking my maker that I decided to go with the sexy lingerie tonight to please Ryker. My dress covers me, though it rises high on my thighs because of my hands. The cool air hits the wet lips of my pussy and I feel wicked and desirable at the same time. I slide them down my legs while Ryker steadies me. I use one of my hands to brace myself on his arm as I step out of my panties and then straighten back up. I tentatively reach out to slop the material into Ryker's waiting hand. They're soaked. My cream has coated them and I should feel embarrassed, but I don't—especially when Ryker brings them up to his face and pushes them against his nose, breathing in my scent. It turns me on in ways I never expected and I feel a fresh gush of wetness. At this rate he's going to make me come and he hasn't even really touched me.

"That's good, Lola. Really good. I think you deserve a reward," he tells me and it takes everything I have not to beg him to take me right then and put me out of my misery, because really that's the only reward I want.

Instead, he pushes my panties into his pocket. It's then I notice the small white box he is carrying. In my excitement and hunger before, I failed to take notice. He opens it and inside is a leather strap. It's beautiful, slim, and delicate despite the material used to make it. It's shiny black with one single silver pendant in the shape of a heart. Inside the heart is also a gold embossed L, standing proudly among a sea of small, shiny stones I know instantly are diamonds. I run my finger along the strip of leather, fingering the diamond heart, but that's not what has my attention. I move my finger along the hand-tooled engraving that has been etched with clear painstaking care. One side says 'Ryker', and on the other side of the heart is the word 'property'.

The words should turn me off, worry me, or at the very least make me send him away. They do none of those things.

"Is this for me?" I ask, unable to believe it. In answer, he turns me around and I move as if in a trance. He stands behind me then and I feel the leather come around my throat.

"It's definitely yours, Lola," he rumbles against my ear as he secures the collar—because instantly some sixth sense tells me that's what it is—around my neck. The weight of it feels heavy, solid...*significant*. "Ask me how long I've had that made, Lola."

"Ryker..."

"Ask me," he instructs again.

"How long?" I ask, almost afraid to hear the answer just in case I'm wrong.

"Since the moment I first saw you as my woman, Lola. You were always mine. I just needed to wait on you to get ready for me," he says.

My breath becomes ragged and before I know what's going on I'm in his truck and he's buckling me in the vehicle before I can form a sane thought.

I'm more than ready now.

CHAPTER 12

Ryker

*W*e've been at the restaurant for the last hour, our food already eaten, and my blood pumping hard and fast through my veins.

When we first entered the restaurant, Lola sat across from me. I didn't say anything to make her move closer, to have her sit right next to me...even if I want her on my fucking lap.

I let her eat in peace, let her get her bearings and get more comfortable. I can see she is nervous and a little scared about what I have planned for her tonight, what I promised I'd do to her.

But I can also see that she is ready, prepared for me.

I feel the weight of her panties in my pocket, still have the smell of her pussy ingrained in my nose, making me drunk. I pick up my beer bottle and take a long drink from it, watching her the whole time. She has her head downcast slightly, but her eyes are trained right on me, her focus right there with mine.

I set the beer bottle down and lean back against the booth. I requested this table in the back of the restaurant, away from prying eyes, from the general population. It gives us some privacy, especially for what I am planning on doing to her.

"Come here, Lola." I don't expect her to disobey me, but I can see the nervousness on her face. She is looking around, maybe worried that somebody will see or hear us. Good. I want the world to know what I do to her, how I make her feel.

"I..."

I can see she wants to maybe argue, wants to go somewhere private, but I also know that if we do this here and now it will be even more exhilarating for her.

"Come here, Lola."

She slips out of the booth and I let my gaze linger on her long legs. The dress she wears is sexy, but also has this touch of innocence to it. I want to see it off her body, tossed on my floor as she lays naked on my bed.

I get up and let her slide into the booth, and then I sit beside her, blocking her in. She is breathing hard, her breasts rising and falling underneath the thin material of the black garment. Her nipples are hard, these little twin erasers that poke against the fabric and have my mouth watering.

Because I am a dirty bastard and am impatient, I shift my body so my back is to the rest of the restaurant. I move my hand so it's now on her thigh and slide it up, pushing the dress up her leg. She feels tense beneath my touch, but her mouth is open and she is breathing hard. Her pupils are also dilated, and as she watches me I know she wants this.

I know she'll be wet as soon as I touch her between her thighs.

"Lean back for me, baby. Let me work you over real good."

"Someone will see, or hear, Ryker." But even as she whispers those words she spreads her legs for me.

I growl low in my throat, the vibrations moving through my chest. I slide my hand toward her sweet spot, and as soon as my fingers touch her soaked folds I make a deep noise in the back of my throat. She makes a small noise and leans back in the booth, giving me full access to her. I stare into her eyes as I start moving my fingers over her cleft and up to her clit. I move the digit over that tiny bundle of nerves.

I lean in even closer to her, our mouths only inches apart. Her breath smells like the vanilla ice cream and strawberries she had for dessert, and I let my tongue run over her bottom lip, tasting that sweetness for myself.

I can feel her shaking, and I work my finger over her clit faster, harder. "Come for me, Lola. Just let go and don't worry about anybody else."

She closes her eyes and moans again, and just as a waitress walks by, oblivious of what I'm doing right now, I move a finger down and tease Lola's pussy hole.

And just like that she comes for me.

She reaches out and places a hand on my thigh, close to my hard dick. She curls her nails into the denim of my pants but I don't stop touching her, don't stop wringing the orgasm from her. She's making little noises, these moans and groans of pleasure that have my cock jerking behind my zipper.

I could come right now just watching the pleasure morph across her face.

And when she finally relaxes I move my hand out from between her thighs, urge her to open her eyes without actually telling her to do so, and hold the glistening fingers I had just been pleasing her with up so she can see them.

Her eyes widen as I bring those digits to my mouth and lick them clean. The groan that spills from me at the flavor of her sweet muskiness has me feeling like a fucking animal.

"Now it's time to go back to my place so I can really show you how you're mine."

CHAPTER 13

Lola

*R*yker puts me in the truck. He doesn't speak, touch me unnecessarily, nor does he kiss me. He buckles my seat belt and closes the door with a loud slam. He does it all without much more than looking at me.

This does nothing to ease the questions and nervousness that begin to barrage my brain. I would love to talk to him. I have questions, concerns, things I would like to ask him, but instead I remain silent—just waiting.

The ride to Ryker's place is quiet. The only sound I can hear in his old truck is my own breathing. It sounds abnormally loud. I have to wonder if he can hear it too. I suppose that should embarrass me, but it doesn't. *Not really.*

I'm pretty sure we will make it to Ryker's place in record time. If I was driving this fast I have no doubt I would get a speeding ticket. We pass several county law vehicles and one state police cruiser. None of them attempt to pull Ryker over.

Maybe they know it is him and are afraid to tangle with the town bad boy?

It would be a wise choice for them to steer clear.

He pulls into his drive so quickly that gravel flies out from around the truck tires. I feel us slide in them and then hear the pinging noises they make as they smack against the undercarriage of the truck. He practically slams on the brakes and I lurch forward in the seat, jarred by the sudden stop. The seatbelt keeps me in place, but I brace my hands on the dashboard to keep from getting whiplash.

He's out of the truck and making his way around the front before I can even contemplate what's going on. I start to unbuckle when Ryker opens the passenger side door and pushes my hands out of the way, taking over completely.

He pulls me straight from the truck and into his arms, not allowing me to walk. I wrap my arms around his shoulders, holding tightly, and do the same with my legs around his hips. I like being this close to him, and having him take care of me in all ways.

"Ryker, stop. I'm too heavy," I finally say, because even if I like him carrying me, it is a little embarrassing. I've never had a man carry me quite like this. In response, his hand slaps hard against my ass, making it jiggle with each step. He growls—an animalistic noise that sends off a multitude of butterflies in the pit of my stomach.

He somehow manages to get the door opened, with me still in his arms. I get a quick glance of the main room of his home. It's surprisingly big. His house is attached to his shop, and I didn't think it would be as spacious as it is. The living room is huge, though sparingly decorated, with just a large black leather couch and a television. It's open to a kitchen,

55

which is similar in size and full of cabinets and a table and chairs.

It's out of sight before I can make note of anything else since he's headed down a dark hallway with me still in his arms. We pass a few doors but at the end of the hall there is an open entryway with a light shining from it. He takes me there and I blink to focus my eyesight just as he puts me down so I can stand on my own.

I keep my hands on his biceps to steady myself and look around. There's a king size, four-post bed off to the side, and a large dresser across from that with a television mounted on the wall above it. That's it. There's nothing else in the room except for a high-back chair that sits directly at the foot of the bed. It's leather and looks like a chair a king would sit in as he greets his subjects. My gaze darts back to Ryker and a chill runs down my spine. I can see him as a king—a conqueror of nations…a conqueror of…*me.*

I take a step away from Ryker. I can't resist looking back at the bed. It's turned down as if waiting for me. The sheets are shiny silk and jet black. They look sinful and remind me so much of Ryker's eyes. I look back up at him—anticipating what is to come. He doesn't make me wait long.

"Undress for me, Lola," he says, his voice dark and commanding.

I swallow down my nerves. Now is not the time to let my nervousness from being a virgin or my fear of the unknown get in the way. I am Ryker's. *I belong to Ryker.* On reflex, my hand comes up to touch the soft leather choker he had made for me. A collar really; I might as well call it what it is. Even in my limited experience I realize exactly what it is. *Realize and embrace it.* I let my finger dance over the embossed 'L' in the center of the collar and I hold Ryker's gaze at the same time. He looks at me as if he is daring me to back out. Does he think I will? The thought that he might think I'm that weak in my conviction leads me to turn around, giving him my back.

"Unzip me?" I ask softly and then because it feels right, feels like something I should give him, I add, "Please, Ryker?"

I'm rewarded by his deep, throaty growl and I know without even having him say anything that I have pleased him. He carefully unzips my dress, but he keeps a hand on my hip, not allowing me to turn back around. Instead, his fingers dance across the small area of skin now exposed. I can feel the hair of his beard gently tickle me and a moment later I feel his gentle kisses. He runs his lips up to the base of my neck. Again his beard tickles the skin and the sensation spreads a fresh wave of goosebumps on my flesh. My eyes close on their own as I feel his teeth rake across the skin, not biting, merely teasing.

Next, I feel his hands in my hair, seeking out the pins I used to pull the strands up. One by one, he begins to release them until my hair is completely down and falling along my shoulders.

"You have beautiful hair, Lola. I want to see it against my sheets. Now, be a good girl and turn around and finish undressing."

I bite my lip to keep from moaning out at how delicious it feels to have Ryker's breath against my skin. I turn around slowly to face him. I take the straps of my dress and slowly lower them, allowing the dress to slide from my body and fall to the floor. I step out of it and force my gaze to lock with Ryker's. It's not easy. I can feel the heat bloom across my skin as I stand before him in nothing but my black lace strapless bra and heels.

"Finish," he commands, his voice hoarse.

Immediately I move my hands up to unhook the clasp between my breasts. My fingers fumble with it, but it releases and I let it fall to the floor. Without thought, I use my arms to cover my breasts. The rest of me is out there. I don't even think to cover my pussy from him, but somehow the cool air against my nipples makes me feel more exposed.

"I…" I start to say something, but the words lodge in my throat when I see the heat in Ryker's gaze. I can almost feel it as if it was a literal touch. His hands come out to capture mine, forcing them away from my body and exposing my breasts completely. I bite back an apology, feeling unsure of myself. I start to bend down to take off my heels, but he stops me.

"Those fucking stay on," he orders. I look up at him, surprised, and watch as he palms his dick through his pants as if he's adjusting himself. The outline of his cock is more than visible against his jeans. I was wet before, feeling my juices painted along my thighs, but seeing the physical effect I have on Ryker just makes me wetter.

"Okay," I murmur, standing back up and suddenly feeling more in control. He might be calling the shots, but I'm the one feeling powerful here.

"Get on the bed on your hands and knees, Lola," he orders. I get on the bed, but freeze when he puts a finger under my chin and pulls my face up to look at him. "Face the headboard," he says and I nod in understanding as he steps back. Once I'm in position, I do my best to steady my breathing. I jerk my head around when I feel Ryker's hand wrap around my ankle.

I watch as he pulls out a silver cuff that is attached to a strap coming from the post on the bed. He connects the cuff around me, and the metal feels cold and foreign. He pulls out my other leg and does the same. I can still remain on my knees, but it's harder; I've had to spread my legs out and I know from where he's standing it opens me even more to him.

"What are...what are you doing?" I ask, unsure if it's okay to question him, but doing it anyway. I look over my shoulder as I hear movement behind me. I see Ryker pick up a box from the dresser.

"Eyes to the front, Lola," he commands, his voice sounding as if he is disciplining me for being bad. I immediately respond, not wanting to displease him further. "Good girl," he approves, stroking my lower back. I'm dying to turn around to see what he's doing, but I don't. I want him to be happy with me. Excitement flushes through me, heating me from the inside out. If he can make me feel like this without actually doing much more than touching me...

"Ryker," I exclaim, when without any type of warning I feel the rough pads of his fingers caress the lips of my wet pussy.

"You're so fucking wet," Ryker growls at the exact moment his fingers find my swollen clit and zero in on it. "So primed for me, so responsive," he adds, and he's right. My body is on fire for him. "You're going to like what happens next, my sweet Lola," he says, kissing the cheek of my ass.

That's the only warning I get before he inserts something

59

between my legs. It's warm and soft…almost gel like. It's also long and thick and it slips between the folds of my pussy and puts pressure against my clit. I go completely still, unsure of what will happen next, when it begins vibrating.

"Ryker," I cry out as sensation immediately begins to crash in on me. My hips move of their own volition as I try to ride the wand that he's torturing me with.

"That's it, Lola. You're going to ride this little beauty while I sit in the chair behind you and watch. You'll do everything I tell you to do, because you want to please me. Won't you, Lola?"

"Ye…yes, Ryker."

"Such a good girl. I'm going to be over here stroking my cock while I watch you. If you do exactly what I tell you, I'll make sure I give you all my cum. Will that make you happy, Lola?"

"Yes. God, yes. I want it, Ryker," I tell him, and I'm already panting, trying to squeeze my pussy so my juices aren't obscenely running down the insides of my legs. But honestly I don't care. I want to come. I want to get off while Ryker covers me in his cum. I see the picture in my mind and I feel dirty and sexy at the same time.

I know the moment he walks away and I can hear him grunt. I know he's stroking his big, hard cock. I thrust my ass back even more, hoping to give him exactly what he wants.

Because I know if I do that, he will give me everything I want —and more.

CHAPTER 14

Ryker

J sit in the chair, kicking my pants off to the side to join my shoes. I grab my t-shirt and pull it over my head to throw it with the rest. Lola is positioned in a way that she can grind herself on the silicone wand I pushed against her pussy.

She has to really work to get it moving through her cunt with her current position, but seeing her move her hips back and forth, all but fucking the hell out of that vibrator, makes me so damn hard I could bust a nut right here and now.

The binds I attached to her ankles still allow her plenty of movement. I won't tighten them until I flip her over and play with her some more. I don't have the willpower to do that without coming first.

I take my cock in my hand, and, holding it at the base, I squeeze tightly to hold back my orgasm. It's either that or come right then and there as I watch how Lola moves faster on the wand, choking it between that sweet pussy. Damn, will she act the same way with my cock? If so, she might break the fucker in two.

"That's it, baby. Ride the fuck out of it. Show me how bad you need my dick," I growl and she cries out my name, a long shudder rolling through her body. She's already close to the edge.

It's that moment that something happens that never has before—*not until Lola*. Suddenly, I don't need to come as much as I need to make her fly apart. I get up and march over to her, covering the small distance quickly.

I move my fingers against her pussy, her sweet cream instantly drowning my digits, coating them. I push against the vibrator, torturing her clit so much more in the process that she cries out and her legs tug against the restraints. I can't wait until the moment I tighten them further so she can't move.

I wonder if she'll scream loudly for me then. Maybe while I'm thrusting my hard cock through her virgin pussy. I groan at the mental image, promising myself it will happen. Her virgin blood will be all over the shaft of my cock and she will own me then, as much as I own her.

"Ryker, I want to come," she whimpers, riding the wand so hard her body is thrusting back and forth.

"Not yet, Lola," I warn, still dragging my fingers through her juices. I hold her hip, forcing her to be still. She cries out in frustration and tries to fight my hold. In answer I lean down and bite one of the plump, juicy globes of her ass. Her entire body shudders for me. I let my tongue slide against the outline of the bite. Fuck, now I want that mark permanently tattooed on her ass. No other fucker will touch her...ever. I'll just have to make sure I do this often. If the way she's throwing her head back and trying to thrust against me is any sign, she likes it, wants a little of that pain.

I take my fingers that are still coated in her sweet cream and push between her cheeks to find the small rosette opening of her ass. I paint it with her cream, smearing it on until the dark area glistens, beckoning me. After I've claimed her pussy, and fixed it so that it's shaped to fit my dick and mine alone, I will be claiming her ass. There won't be a hole on her body I haven't taken and made my own. *Fuck that.* There won't be a part of *her* that won't have my ownership written across it. Lola is mine and I'll kill the first asshole who says differently.

I use my other hand to smear my fingers along her pussy again right before dipping back into her cunt, purposely shifting the wand so that it hits her clit at a different angle. Lola lets out a high, keening cry. Maybe she's beyond words at this point, her breathing so loud it sounds like music to my ears as it echoes in the room loudly.

I take my fingers that are soaked in her sweet pussy juice and, without even trying to be gentle, I push them into her ass. It's so fucking tight I have to shove them in almost violently, but nothing will stop me from claiming everything about her. Once I push through the small ring of muscles, I let my fingers separate, widening her opening. I must have been wrong because it's that moment Lola gives me something I didn't even ask for.

She goes down low on her arms, her head touching the mattress. The action pushes her ass out higher in the air and the whole pose is one of surrender. That is fucking hot enough, but then she makes it even better.

"Ryker, Ryker, Ryker..." She repeats my name over and over like a prayer—or as if she's looking for me to save her, to answer her plea.

That's what finally drives me to fuck her ass with my fingers, pushing them in and out, first slow but steady and then faster, as I use my hand to take over her body and dictate her thrusts. She moves on the vibrator like a rodeo queen, fucking herself like she's riding a thoroughbred at the Derby.

Jesus, I can't wait until my cock is inside of her. I can already feel pre-cum running down my cock. We're both too fucking close to the edge. For that reason—and that reason alone—I finally decide to take pity on her. Although if I'm completely honest, I might be doing it because I can't stop myself. Lola destroys my control completely.

I remove the wand from her, shutting it off and tossing it to the other side of the bed.

"No!" she cries out, her entire body fighting against the loss. I shift my position, taking my fingers away and slapping her ass in warning all at the same time. "Ryker!" she cries, drawing out my name. Still, even with the protest, her body stills when I deliver her spanking.

I pull on her thighs, widening her stance, and then slide under her body. With very little encouragement and limited direction using my hold on her, she adjusts until she's sitting on my face. Her clit is throbbing against my lips, hard and engorged. I flick it with my tongue, burying my face in that sweet pussy. I eat her like a man starving, pushing my face into her warm depths. I shove my tongue deep into her sweet spot, licking against her inner walls. My cock, which is already as hard as concrete, grows impossibly thicker. She's so fucking close to getting off she tries to squeeze against my face, riding the ridge of my nose, bathing me in her sweetness.

I hear her crying out above me, and for a moment I wonder if I can keep her like this, torturing her over and over until she comes so hard she loses consciousness. I'd be willing to try it if I wasn't so close to the edge myself. So instead, I slide my fingers back into her ass, pushing the digits deep inside at the same time I capture her clit between my teeth and apply a gentle pressure. In that moment she climaxes, and I lick it all up.

Every. Fucking. Drop.

CHAPTER 15

Ryker

"*P*lease," she whispers.

"Please what?" I murmur against her swollen, soaked folds.

"Fuck me."

I groan deeply. Yeah, I'll fuck her all right. "You want me to pop that cherry of yours?"

She nods. "God, yes. Now. Please." And then she moans and thrusts her pussy against my face. I want to fuck her so damn badly, but I keep torturing us. I start rubbing her pussy lips, sliding my fingers toward her center, and run the digits up and down her slit.

She grinds herself on me even harder, more frantic. I know I could get her off again but I want her to come on my cock, with me buried deep inside of her. I work my fingers along her pussy lips, the silky smoothness of her flesh so fucking hot I know I won't last once I'm balls deep in her cunt.

I pull away, regretfully moving from the bed, but only long enough to take the ties off her ankles. I give her ass some hard slaps, growl at the way she cries out, and flip her onto her back. When I move up her body, letting my cock slide along her upper thigh, my pre-cum coating her skin, I envision myself marking her up real good. I start thrusting my dick against her belly, the friction feeling fucking fantastic.

I could come just from the motion alone.

And I want to get off, but I'll be deep in her body when that happens.

"How much do you like it, baby? How much do you want this?"

"God, Ryker, I want it so much."

I move my other hand that wasn't just ass-fucking her between our bodies and find her clit, rubbing my thumb over the bud back and forth, harder and faster.

"I want to be deep inside of you. I want to be so far up in you all you can think about is me." I start licking and nipping at her neck, loving the saltiness that forms because she's starting to sweat from this. I'm giving her a hard workout and this is only the beginning. "I want my cock in your cunt, want to feel your pussy milking me, strangling my dick." I stroke her clit faster, harder, and suck her skin with more force, knowing there will be a mark…needing there to be one.

She starts moving her hips, grinding her pussy on my hand, clearly wanting to get off. And hell, I want her to come.

But I need to be inside of her first.

JORDAN MARIE & JENIKA SNOW

Removing my hand, I lift it so she can see how glossy my fingers are. "Open your mouth." She does without hesitation, and it makes me so fucking turned on my balls hurt. "Suck on them." She opens her mouth and I push my fingers between her lips, watching as she does what I say.

"You taste good, don't you?"

She nods.

I lift my digits to my mouth and suck on them too, groaning at how good she fucking tastes.

I'm done with the foreplay. I need to have my cock deep in her.

I need to make her mine.

"I'm going to pound my cock so hard into your pussy, so raw, so possessively, you'll feel it tomorrow when you sit down." I am such a filthy fucking bastard, but fuck, she likes it. I know she does. "You'll feel that soreness, that tenderness from having my huge dick in you, and you'll know you're *mine*."

Yeah, she'll feel every last inch of me tomorrow, hell, for the next several days. I'll pound my cock deep in her body so there is no doubt in her mind who she belongs to. And any motherfucker who thinks they can challenge me for her, who tries to tell me Lola isn't mine in all ways, will find out swiftly what it is like to get their ass kicked by me.

* * *

Lola

I FEEL LIKE ANOTHER PERSON, like this really isn't me participating in this wanton, erotic act. I don't want to be the virgin

68

who doesn't know what is going to happen. I want to be experienced so I can give Ryker exactly what he is about to give me.

Then do it. Jump outside of the preconceived notions that you have to be the shy virgin. Tell him what you want.

"I need you in me," I finally manage to say, forcing myself to be the woman I've always wanted to be with him.

The sound he makes is of a man losing what little control he has left. I'm flipped over onto my belly a second later, the air leaving me.

He parts my ass cheeks, slides his fingers between my thighs, and I gasp at the sensation of his thick fingers moving through my soaked flesh.

"You're so fucking wet for me, so ready for me to break in this virgin pussy, aren't you, baby girl?"

I can only nod.

"I can't wait any longer to tear you up. I have to break this cherry and make it my own. I have to watch as your cunt swallows my dick whole."

A second later I feel the head of his dick press against my entrance.

In one swift move he buries all of his monstrous inches into me. I feel my eyes widen, feel like I'm splitting in two. Tears prick the corner of my eyes, and I suck in a breath. I am stretched fully. The burn is there, the discomfort instant. He slowly pulls out and pushes back in. He is so big and long, so thick and completely consuming me.

I look over my shoulder at him. Every muscle I can see on him is taut, and his face is strained. I feel his hands tighten painfully on my waist, and I know I'll get exactly what I want soon enough.

He doesn't give me time to adjust to his size, doesn't give me a chance to think about what is going on. He starts fucking me then. Ryker pulls out so just the tip is lodged in my pussy, then shoves deep in me. He does it so hard, so fast I feel the air leave me. My inner muscles clench rhythmically around his monstrous cock.

"You feel so fucking good."

He fucks me like this for long seconds, but then pulls out before we can really get this going. In the next moment he has me turned around so I'm facing him. He runs his hands down my inner thighs, frames my pussy, and for a second just stares at me.

"All mine," he says and grabs his cock. I look down and see my wetness and blood covering the length. The virgin redness is streaked on his impressive cock, and I feel my inner muscles clench.

He aligns his cock with my pussy again, and while holding my gaze, he thrusts in deep once more. As the seconds move, his motions become more frenzied. He is like a madman between my legs, making these grunts and growls that remind me of a wild animal.

All I can do is hold on and let him fuck me.

"You like my big cock between your thighs, my fingers digging into you, don't you, Lola baby?" He slams inside of me, and I gasp.

"God, yes."

He groans. "You're so fucking tight and wet."

"God, yes." I can only repeat the same words. Thinking is beyond me. My words are high-pitched as they spill from me. The sound of his cock moving in and out of my pussy is loud, dirty in a good way.

I am about to come, but he slows and leans forward, licking my breasts, the stiff peaks hardening under his tongue. And all the while he continues to work his dick in and out of me.

"As much as I fucking love watching my cock slide in and out of your cunt, your body craving mine, I want to see the pleasure on your face when you come all over my dick."

God, I get off for him again.

"God, fuck yes," he grunts against my mouth, and starts slamming his dick into me then.

And then somehow I come again, just let go, fall over the edge. I can't even breathe.

"*Christ*, baby girl, you're so fucking hot. You're so damn wet my cock is soaked."

He pulls out slightly and then slams back into me hard. I cry out at how intensely good it feels.

"I'll never get enough," he says, and although this is the first time we've been together, I can't help but believe him. "I want you to ride me until you're bouncing on my cock, until you get so wild you're sore tomorrow."

"Oh. God," I whisper. The next second I am shifted and he is under me. My legs are spread over his hips, my pussy almost aligned with his cock head.

"Fuck me, baby. Put my cock deep in your pussy and ride me."

And I do just that. Once his cock is lodged deep in my body, I start rocking back and forth on him. I rest my hands on his pecs, bracing myself. I start bouncing on him, up and down, harder and faster.

"*Christ.*" His voice is rough, his hold on me fierce.

Everything in me tightens. He stretches me so good, and

71

the burn of the pleasure is still there. I never want it to end. My breath leaves me and my arms shake from holding myself up, but still I ride him.

"You're mine. All fucking mine."

I am his. All his.

I don't want this to ever end.

CHAPTER 16

Lola

*T*hree days. That's all it's been since I've been in Ryker's bed, but it feels like forever. It feels like my life has always been this wonderful. Ryker took my virginity three days ago and I'm completely his. Everything is better. Tonight is my first night back to work. Ryker wasn't happy. He doesn't want me working here. I told him no one would dare mess with me now—not when word has gotten out that I belong to him. He still doesn't like it. Somehow I convinced him to let me come to work tonight, but only on the condition that I stay inside the bar, let one of the others take out the garbage and that he brings me and picks me up. Since I really don't want to be without him, I agreed easily.

He dropped me off with a kiss that melted me and left me hungry for more. He had to go back to work at the shop, but he promised to be back before time for me to get off. I'm about an hour from my shift being done and there's still been no sign of him. I miss him; my body misses him. Maybe he was right and I should quit work. If I wasn't working, I could be at his garage right now. He offered me a job in his office. I could do that and see him all the time…maybe even beg him to fuck me on my desk…

For a woman that three days ago had never had sex, it seems to be all I can think about now. I know instinctively it's because it was Ryker. It's because I am his—and he is mine. He's ruined me for other men, and he seems to have no interest in other women either. He tells me I'm the one he's been waiting for and… *I believe him.*

"Lola, we need to talk." I turn around quickly. I hate that voice. *My mother.* When she's around trouble is bound to be close behind.

"I can't talk right now. I'm working."

"Working," she scoffs. "Why do you need to work? Word around town is that you've managed to capture Ryker Stone's attention. Was it all a lie?"

"I… That's none of your business, really, Mother," I tell her, not liking the idea of my mom spending any time whatsoever thinking about my relationship with Ryker. There are people in this world that are just toxic and my mother is definitely one of those. I don't want her near anything that Ryker and I share.

I'm so lost in my thoughts that I don't see her hand coming toward me. I cry out when it connects with the side of my face, the burning sting of pain following the hit swiftly.

"You don't talk to me like that! I am your mother!" she cries out.

"You touch my woman again, and the only thing you will

be is planted in the ground for the worms to devour," Ryker growls out, his voice colder than anything I've ever heard. It chills me and I know without a shadow of a doubt he would never hurt me. "Lola, come here," he orders and I walk to him, still holding my cheek. He pulls my hand down to inspect my face. I can't know what he sees, but I feel the glowing heat from the hit still, and I can tell from the anger vibrating through him, and showing on his stern face, that it's not good. "Slim!" he yells out, his gaze never leaving mine.

"Yeah, Ryker?" my boss answers.

"What the fuck are you doing here? You can't protect my woman one night? First she almost gets gang-raped out back last week and now this. Where the fuck are your bouncers?"

"Man, they've been watching for other men, but well... Shit, man, it's her mom."

"That woman is nothing but a piece of trash to take out," Ryker growls and I don't disagree with him. She's never been a mother. I actually have to wonder why she showed up here.

I shouldn't have worried, though. She makes the reason abundantly clear with her next screeching statement.

"Who the hell do you think you are? Calling me trash like that! I'm her mother! I fed and clothed the ungrateful piece of shit year after year! She owes me!" she hisses and my eyes go big. I started work at sixteen and even before that I mostly ate at one of the neighbors' trailers in the park we lived at. My mother never gave a shit about me.

"What exactly do you think—" I start to respond, but Ryker doesn't let me. He crosses in front of me protectively. My mouth shuts closed, because it's apparent Ryker doesn't want me dealing with her.

"What is it you want from her?" Ryker says, getting to the heart of the matter.

"I think this discussion is better had between me and Lola."

"Lady, you are crazy if you think you are getting anywhere near my woman again. Now, my patience is wearing thin. I want to take my woman home, make sure she is okay and then get lost deep inside of her and go to sleep. You are keeping me from that. So spit out exactly why you crawled out from under your rock and let's be done with it."

"I would rather speak with Lola," she argues stubbornly.

"And we're done here," Ryker says, turning away from her and back to me.

"I need money!"

"What the fuck?" Ryker mutters. He looks at me and, despite the still burning pain of my cheek, I know the color drains from my face. It's one thing to know your mother is a bitch who could care less about you; it's quite another to let the man you love see it. I want Ryker to see me as someone worthy of love—someone he could be proud of.

What if he thinks because she is my mother that I will end up being just like her?

"Ryker—" I start, but he doesn't let me finish. For a second I'm scared this will cause him to leave me. Then he turns back around to my mother.

"I'm listening," he snarls out.

"I need to get out of town. I'm going to California."

"What does that have to do with Lola?"

"I need some money to get out of here."

"How in the hell is that our problem?"

"It's not yours! But Lola is my daughter and she owes me!

76

She's got a job and now you. Everyone in this godforsaken town knows you're loaded. The least she can do is give me enough money to help me start over!"

"How exactly does she owe you?"

"She stole years of my life! She's the reason Phillip left me!"

"Who the hell is Phillip?" Ryker barks.

"Her last boyfriend," I whisper, feeling sick to my stomach.

"Then he probably left because he couldn't handle waking up to a rack of bones that stays doped up out of her mind," Ryker justifies.

"He left because of Lola!"

"I doubt—"

"He left because I told him the next time he tried to break into my room and climb in my bed I'd have him arrested!" I defend, sick of all of this, and mostly sick that this person is my mother.

"He what?" Ryker asks, his voice deadly.

"You should have just let him. Phillip was good to you. You didn't complain when he put food on the table," my mother claims, like she's tired of talking about it.

"You aren't getting a penny from Lola or from me," Ryker says and this time he's not yelling at my mother. He's not growling in his normal tone. This time his voice is deadly quiet and has the strength of steel behind it.

"She—"

"We don't really know each other, so I'm going to give you advice now. Lola is mine. She saved herself for me. You just told her she should have given what was mine away. More than that, you just admitted you would have sacrificed your innocent daughter to keep your man happy since you couldn't."

"How dare you!"

"This is the only warning you get, so you better heed my advice, lady, because I'm not giving it twice. You leave this place and you don't even try to contact Lola again. As far as you are concerned she's dead to you."

"You don't have that right."

"I have every right. I'm protecting my woman from a viper like you."

"You have no control over me. I'm not some lapdog like you're trying to turn my daughter into."

"I can see you're not going to listen to my warning. So let me tell you what will happen if you don't leave. That fucking candy store you've been running out of the trunk of your car will be discovered. I'll make sure enough fuckwads come forward to pin your ass to the wall."

"You can't. You don't have the proof to do that."

"It's amazing what money can do, and as you just said… I'm loaded. So try me. I'll make sure they lock you in a federal pen with security so tight you'll never see the light of day."

My mother is watching Ryker closely. I can see the moment she knows she's hit a wall she can't get around. I even see a glimpse of real fear on her face.

I don't know what she would have said next. I don't get the chance to ask.

Ryker spins around and picks me up, throwing me over his shoulder in a fireman's carry so fast my head spins. I cry out and try to steady myself by using my hands on his back.

"Slim?"

"Yeah, Ryker?"

"My woman quits. She's going to work at the garage where I know she's safe and filth can't touch her."

"You got it, man," I hear Slim answer right before the door to the club slams behind us.

Ryker marches over to his old truck like a man with a purpose. He opens the door and then shifts me so I'm standing.

"Do you have a problem with anything that happened in there, Lola?" he asks.

"No," I answer honestly.

"Good. Then I'm taking you back home, I'm fucking you raw and then after I've calmed down, I'll fuck you soft. You got anything to say to that?"

"Take me home, Ryker," I whisper softly.

He grunts in reply, scoops me up and deposits me in the seat of his truck and buckles me in. He's still vibrating with anger at my mother, but even in his fury he takes the time to kiss my lips. He kisses them softly, too, letting none of his anger bleed through.

With Ryker I know I'll always be safe. It's such a beautiful feeling.

EPILOGUE

Ryker

One year later

For me there is only Lola. There will only ever be Lola.

Until she came into my life I didn't know I could actually be happy, that a bastard like me deserved something so pure and good.

A year has already passed since I staked my claim on her. I made her quit that fucking bar job, and told her whatever she wanted to do I'd support her. And now she is enrolled in some community classes and loving the hell out of it.

I pull into the driveway and cut the engine. I'm out of the truck and in the house, anxious to see her, in a few minutes flat. She's in the kitchen, the smell of steak filling my nose. My woman might be younger than me, but fuck, does she know how to cook her man a meal.

With her back to me I walk up to her, my dick already hard, my need for her never dimming in this last year. Hell, I fuck her nearly every day simply because I can't get enough of her sweet fucking pussy.

I reach out, wrap my hand around her waist, and spin her around. She gasps and falls into me, and I let out a pleasurable growl as her taut breasts press against my chest. I grind my cock into her belly and she hums in approval. She's always ready for me, her pussy always soaked for my big dick.

Her mom is no longer in the picture. And even though the bitch had started shit was us a year ago, I was glad she wasn't messing with what Lola and I had anymore. She knows better. No fucking way I'll let her fuck things up.

I lower my face to her neck and inhale deeply. "You wet for me, baby girl?"

She sighs her answer. I run the tip of my nose up the side of her throat, loving the smell of her. She makes this sweet little moan and presses closer to me.

"You smell like you've been working all day."

"What, all of a sudden you don't like the smell of a garage on your man?" I tease.

"I love it."

Yeah, she does.

As much as I want to fuck her, I need to get serious.

Really fucking serious.

"You okay?"

"I'll be right back." I leave her alone for a second and head into the bedroom to get the engagement ring box I hid there. Once back to where she is, I drop to one knee, not about to prolong this, and hoping I don't fuck it up.

When I show her the box her eyes widen. "I can make this long as fuck, try and woo you, show you I can be a gentleman, but the truth is you love me for the gruff bastard I am." I cup the side of her face again. "I love you so damn much." I open the box and show her the ring. "You're the only woman I want to spend my life with, to be big and pregnant with my babies." I slip the diamond on her ring finger. "Will you marry me?"

She doesn't say anything for a few seconds, but the happiness is clear on her face. "Yes. Always. Forever."

I pull her into my embrace and hold her tight, never letting go. She's mine, always has been, and always will be.

The End

Breaking Dragon
Savage Brothers MC Series
Book 1
Jordan Marie

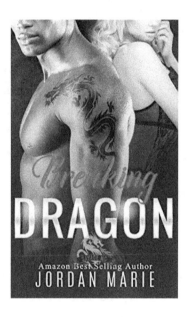

Chapter 1

Nicole

It's Sunday. That shouldn't be a momentous thing because you get one of those every week, if you're lucky enough to survive. Still it is. It is because today is the day that Dani and I are picking up the last of our boxes and moving out of Blade. Blade, Kentucky was a small hole in the wall with less than one hundred people living there. Bet you didn't know places like that existed, did you? Well they do. We have a city hall, one bank, a gas station-outlet tobacco store and a volunteer fire department. That's the grand total of all the buildings in Blade. The few kids that live in Blade are driven by their parents to a school one county over. I've lived here my entire life and even though it may sound like it, I'm not really complaining. I love Blade. It's living near my parents I don't enjoy.

My parents really shouldn't have settled down here. After all, there are no country clubs, no private dining facilities, none of the amenities befitting their station. Yes, that is sarcasm you detect. Those are words I've heard a million times coming from my mother's lips; lips that had never kissed the top of my head when I was sad, nor spoke words of encouragement when I failed, lips that have been painted deep ruby red for as long as I could remember, and brought to mind a cold and lifeless corpse.

You might be realizing there is no love lost between my mother and me—you would be right. The simple truth is my parents remain in Blade because my dad, Marcus Samuel Wentworth the second, owns the sole bank in the city and the one in the neighboring area of Burkesville. Here, my parents are important, specifically my mother. If she moved away, she would lose that distinction, and Gwyneth couldn't handle that. Father too for that matter, he was a step or two up from mother dear, but that's not really saying much. Sometimes, I wonder how I could be their daughter. I would have thought I was adopted except for my hair. The dirty-blonde hair I have is the same color as my mother's. For that reason alone, I put dark caramel color through it, darkening it so now it looks nothing like hers. She hated it. I celebrated it.

I'm getting all dragged down talking about the parental units. That's enough to depress me and that can't happen on this awesome day. Today, Dani and I are moving to London, Kentucky. See? Momentous!

Okay, well it isn't that far away to be honest, but it is at least three hours and that's good for now. It's a two bedroom house on the outskirts of the city and it'll be far away from my parents. Dani and I have jobs. I'm going to be a waitress at the Wolves Den, she will be dancing. I'd never have the nerve to dance for several reasons. First, Dani makes me brave, but she can't make me believe I don't have mega flaws. Dani is drop dead gorgeous. Me? That's reason number two, I have boobs that are a little too large, and my ass is just a tad too wide. My thighs aren't my favorite thing ever. I'm a size fourteen. I'll never fit into Dani's size eights. I used to want to, but as I got older I decided I like who I am well enough. So screw it. Plus, I'm pretty outspoken at times, but I'm way too freaking shy to be a dancer. My girl makes me brave, but there's not anyone able to make me brave enough to bare my boobs and ass to a bunch of strangers. It's going to be hard enough getting used to the mini booty shorts and black tank that shows way too much of the aforementioned boobs, but I'm determined.

I want to branch out into real life and live. So I've made the decision to not let my conscience get the better of me and just experience the different things that are out there. It's silly, and a decision that may bite me in the ass.

I've never really been the type to want to go to college. That's an issue my parents bring up regularly—as just another one of my failures among a long list. I've never really had aspirations to do something with my life other than enjoy it. Maybe I'll make plans later on. I don't know and frankly at twenty-four I probably should, but I don't really care right now. It took too long to break away from Blade. I'll figure it out as I go along.

"Woo!!!!!!!!!!!!!!" Dani hollers, as we're speeding down the interstate in my convertible Mercedes.

Her hands are waving in the air and I can't help but laugh over the pounding of the radio. I love my car. It's a shit hot baby blue Mercedes E350 Convertible, and it's the only thing my parents gave me that I love. It's the last gift they gave me. It was when I was graduating from high school and they still thought they had a chance of molding me into who they thought I should be. Luckily, it was in my name and paid for when they gave me the keys. One month later, they found out I wouldn't be going to college to find myself a future doctor or lawyer as a husband. Yes, that was the reason given for why I should enroll in college. I refused, and then I was pretty much cut off. Luckily, I had Dani. She had always been there for me. We are as different as night and day and honestly, there is no *reason* why Dani and I are friends. Some things just happen. Dani walks to the beat of her own drum. She is a force of nature, a hurricane, a category five hurricane. She inspires me. She scares me. She makes me happy. I love her. She took me in and I lived with her and her brother Roy, who was a nice guy and cute as hell. Too bad he was also gay. That was just my luck.

We did okay there, working to save every bit of money we could until we had enough to make a big move. Three hours away might not be a big move for some, but it sure as hell was for us. We pooled our money and had the rent paid for three months, plus the safety deposit. We now have enough to stock the fridge good and live and pay utilities until we get paid from our new jobs. Roy has a friend who worked as a manager for Wolves Den and got us interviews. We nailed the jobs and told them we needed two weeks to give our former employers notice. We didn't really, but it takes time to move and get settled. It happened so quickly once we made the decision, that my head is still kind of dizzy, but I'm happy. I look over at my best friend for life and smile—really happy.

"Hey, I'm thirsty!" Dani hollers.

"We're just thirty minutes or so away!" I yell back, not crazy about stopping.

"Big damn deal, let's get some drinks and chocolate girl!" She yells back.

I frown and look down at my gas gauge. I could use some gas. I give my signal to get over and take the upcoming exit. We have to take it to get to where our new home will be. So off I go. We pull into the first gas station I see. I cut the engine off and push my hands through my hair shaking it out, because hello, interstate driving, convertible. Enough said.

"Whatcha' want bitch?" Dani asks, and I laugh at her. She's yelling over the music. Ludacris is blasting through the speakers.

"Pepsi, fountain if they have it," I yell back, looking around. I notice there are a bunch of men on bikes by the entrance. They're looking over at us laughing. I open the door, cutting off Ludacris as he screams out about his woman riding his dick. I can feel the heat rising up in my face and turn my eyes from them immediately. Shit!

Our "on the road" play list is very eclectic and the Ludacris' offering is one of Dani's choices. Don't get me wrong, I like it. I like a bit of naughty and I like the beat, but it's not my usual thing. Lorde's song Team is next. That's me, but what the hell. I don't know the men that are laughing, maybe they aren't even laughing at me. It feels like they are though. I hate this about me. I am so self-conscious I automatically take things personally and find myself lacking. Dani isn't like that. She'd flip the bikers off and go about her business. I wanted to be like that. I have just never achieved it. They are laughing harder now, but I turn around to the pump and run my card through and ignore them. In my mind I'm wondering if my ass is hanging out of my cut offs and if that's why they are laughing. Can they see the small catsup stain on my pink shirt from the fries we had shared in the car earlier? I set the pump to go on its own and start cleaning the trash out of the car. I'm mostly trying to keep myself busy and ignoring the bikers. It takes a while; my conclusion is that my girl and I are pigs.

I walk over to the garbage can and throw the crap in. When a deep gravelly voice from behind me sends chills up my back.

"Damn I've heard of it, but I don't think I've ever seen it." I turn slowly and look up to see one of the bikers standing in front me. I bite my lip and move back a small step. I ground my teeth into one corner of my lip and my hands go to the back pockets of my shorts as I take him in, and damn there is a lot to take in. Holy Mother of God, standing before me is a man that towers over me. He's at least a good six foot. His mocha skin glistens in the sun and he's wearing a black t-shirt that's worn to the point it's almost gray, over that he has on a leather vest. Weird, because it's like eighty freaking degrees today, but I can't deny it's sexy. I think maybe he could wear a feed sack and it'd be sexy.

The vest has the word Savage written on it in dark red letters and underneath a rabid wolf. It's kind of scary looking. Underneath that is the word President. I move my eyes up from his massive chest and the biceps covered in tattoo's, to look into the most gorgeous eyes I have ever seen in my life. They are a deep, dark, sparkling brown, and I think I could drown in them and be happy. His hair is cut short to his head with just enough left that I want to see how the texture would feel against my skin.

I let go of my lips and lick them because my whole mouth has gone dry.

The god before me would be a good way to let go and experience life.

Bad Nicole whispers in my head, and the sane part of me agrees. I wouldn't mind a piece of what stands before me, not that I'd ever have a chance of holding onto him, but still.

"What's that?" I ask and shit does my voice sound breathless.

"A barefoot Kentucky girl." he says.

I look down at my feet, realizing I left my flip flops in the car. I hate shoes and I absolutely hate driving with shoes on. I tend to wrap my toes around the pedals of a car and you can't do that with shoes on. I forget to put them back on all the time. I once went to the grocery store and got all the way to the door, before I noticed I was barefoot.

I look back at him and turn my head to the side in what I hoped was a flirty action.

"You must be new to Kentucky." I'm feeling warm all over; can he see the heat rising on my face?

"No Mama. Been here awhile, seen a lot of girls in a lot of places. Don't believe I've ever seen one pumping gas barefoot."

"Glad I could be your first." I grin, wondering if he could pick up on the sexual innuendo. I'm subtle, way too subtle sometimes, as Dani likes to remind me constantly.

His lush, full lips widen into a smile and his bright white teeth are visible for a minute. It's a good smile. Damn good.

"What's your name Twinkie?" He asks. The boys with him laugh harder. I don't know why, maybe it was just a sixth sense, but I don't think I like that name. Now when he had called me Mama? I'm pretty sure I drenched my panties.

"Does it matter?" I ask, a little confused with the situation coming at me.

"I like to know the name of the woman who took my virginity." He quips, his long arm leaning against the post by the gas pump.

Guess that means he picked up on my innuendo. Only now with his boys laughing, I get the feeling this is some kind of game, and that disappoints me. I have been the butt of too many jokes, way too often, mostly because of my size.

The pump kicks off and I reach down to take the nozzle out when he does it for me. His hand brushes mine. I feel a charge of electricity at that small touch and my nipples harden in reaction. Damn, that has never happened before and this guy was the wrong person for it to be happening with.

"How about you just call me mystery, that way you won't get me confused with the millions of girls that come after me," I smile, though it probably didn't reach my eyes, but he wouldn't know that.

"Damn Nic, when I said I wanted chocolate, you didn't have to go all out bitch. Hello there, Tall Dark and Do me all over." Dani pipes up, as I close the gas lid and shake my head.

I turn back around to see him look Dani up and down and I don't miss the interest flair in his eyes. I sigh, yep, no competing with Dani. I take my pop from her hand while she is still staring at Stud Muffin.

"Dani meet Stud, Stud meet Dani. I popped his cherry while you were in the store," I say walking around to the driver's side of the car. The men laugh harder, I continue to ignore them. Dani laughs and opens the door, careful not to hit him as she gets in; I notice he closes her door. Damn. Yeah, that's jealousy I feel, dang it. Stud doesn't move away either. His hands are firmly propped on the passenger door and he leans in the window. Damn Dani and her sexy size eights. Still, when I look up, his eyes are on me.

"Me and my crew," he said, and jerks his head in the direction of the men who had finally stopped laughing, "are having a party this Tuesday. You girls should come. It's the least you can do for stealing my virginity and all Nicole. I was saving that," he said, stressing my name to let me know he had it now.

"Sorry Stud, we just moved and have some stuff to do before we start work Friday." I reply, starting up the car. Immediately, Ludacris fills the air again, but I reach down and mute it quickly.

"Where are you working?" He asks, looking straight at

me, and I wonder if for a minute I mistook his interest in Dani, but then I realize he's sizing us both up. He's a player, a total player—disappointing, but not surprising.

"Wolves Den," I say putting the car in drive, but I keep my foot on the brake. His smile grows and he walks around the front of the car and slaps the hood.

"Maybe I'll see you around sometime then Twinkie."

"Sorry, I don't do repeats, it's hard to beat that first time." I reply waiting for him to move past the hood so I can go on.

"Now that's damned disappointing. Maybe I can show you some things get better with practice," he purrs.

"It's nice you believe in miracles. Good to know I didn't take all your innocence," I return. He barely clears my car before I give it some gas and pull out from the pumps, intent on getting away.

"Be seeing you soon."

I ignore that warning, and the chills it sends down my spine, and turn the sound back up on my radio. By this time Creep from Radiohead, is on so I crank it high.

"Who the hell was that?" Dani asks when we get on the road, turning my music back down.

"Have no idea. Thought he was sexy, but he seemed to be getting his jollies off messing with me, while his buddies laughed."

Dani was silent, but I saw her nod out of the corner of my eye.

We go down the road about a mile or so before I notice the bikes behind us. I can see Stud in the back mirror with his shades covering his eyes. Damn he is sex on a stick.

"Don't look now, but I think your play toy is following you." Dani says looking through her side mirror. I turn on the signal to cut down road 80, where the house we had rented is located. I couldn't help but notice the bikes followed.

"Do you think we should be worried?" I ask, trying not to hyperventilate.

"Nah, it's a long road, maybe they live on it, or maybe he just wants to tap your ass. Worse things could happen girl. Hell, it's been forever since you got laid."

She's not wrong. I had been with two other guys. One was in high school. I was sixteen and gave my virginity to my boyfriend Marshall after prom. Both Marshall and the giving away of my virginity were a mistake. The second was the last relationship I was in, Tony or as I affectionately referred to him, Tony the Tool. I sucked the big one at picking men.

We drive a little further along the road then turn up a dirt road on the right. It leads to the house we rented. We'd found an ad online and rented it just by the pictures. Apparently the pictures were old because the grass out front would come up past my knees. Holy Splendor in the Grass, Batman!

"Shit." Dani said, and I wholeheartedly agree as we pull into the drive. I park and we get out, still in shock.

We hear the bikes following us in, somehow I'm not surprised, but I am in shock over the house, so my attention is somewhat diverted. I am counting up the hours I'll be stuck doing yard work and praying the house is in better shape, when Tall, dark and studly parks his bike beside me.

"Nice place, Twinkie." He says and at least this time the boys aren't laughing.

I turn so I can face him. God he is hot. Did I forget to mention that? Even if I didn't, it sure as hell needs repeating.

"Listen it's cute how you cling to me and everything, but

first rule in cherry popping 101, hit it and quit it. So really we should say goodbye now." I hear Dani snort over his men's laughter.

"You go barefoot in these weeds Mama and you're liable to get snake bit."

I roll my eyes. "I have shoes, plus last time I checked I was a big girl, you don't need to worry Daddy." I open the car door, get out my flip flops and put them on my feet.

I am giving him much more lip than I normally would. I'm not sure why, but I think it is because it felt like he and his men were laughing at me earlier. If you added that along with the fact he checked out Dani, of whom I could never compete with, while I was standing right there....

"I've never liked that before," he says resignedly, getting off his bike.

I take a step back now that he is standing beside me. I had to, to try and get air or I would have swooned. It was a near miss as it was.

"What's that?" I ask suddenly lost to the conversation.

"Being called Daddy, but it might be hot as hell from you. Especially, if you scream it out while I'm spanking that ass of yours."

Have you ever seen a goldfish jump out of its bowl and flap around? Its mouth opening and closing while it's trying desperately to breathe? I'm pretty sure that's what I look like.

Then he shocks me further by picking me up and walking me towards the house.

"Wait! What on earth are you doing?"

"Mama those things on your feet are cute as hell, but they aren't going to protect you from snakes." I hear Dani laughing and looked over Stud's shoulders to see her piggy back riding one of the other men. She was having the time of her life; I am confused, aroused and panicked. See? Totally different from Dani, damn it!

"Put me down! I'm too heavy," I say, feeling way out of my depth here. I had never been literally picked up by a man before, but especially by a man I didn't even know. At my words, he shifts and turns me so I am hanging half over his back. His hand comes up and slaps me hard on the ass.

"Ow! What the hell was that for?"

"Quit talking about yourself like that. You sure as hell aren't heavy."

"I don't even know you, you creep. What the hell do you think you're doing?"

"Spanking an ass I plan on tapping later?" *Gulp!* I think this might be an Oh-shit-moment if ever there was one. What did you say to that? I mean I didn't even know him!

JUMP HIM!

Bad Nicole orders in my head. She seems to be coming out to play more and more around this man, and I only met him thirty minutes ago! If that!

"There's no way in hell!" I growl, as he puts me down on the small cement square in front of the back door.

Liar! Bad Nicole chided.

I really need to find a way to slap that bitch.

"Oh yeah there is Mama, and something else you should know, before I'm through you're going to be begging me to spank you harder."

My face jerks back like he had hit me. Seriously? Did he just say that to me? I would have argued, but he picks that moment to grab me by the back of the head and pull me to him. My hands come up between us, to try and pull away. He is too strong, or I didn't really try—one of those. He slams his lips against mine. He slides his mouth over mine possessively. I grind my teeth together refusing to open for him. His tongue teases along the inside of my bottom lip. It feels good. It feels divine, yet somehow I had the wherewithal to not open my mouth.

Because you're stupid!

Bad Nicole should seriously go back into hibernation.

Stud must have got impatient. I can feel his hand moving between us. It leaves a heated path though my shirt along my stomach, his touch is gentle, but oh so commanding. I would be lying if I didn't admit my resistance is melting. It so was, but in the end that didn't matter. His hand reaches up to my chest and he places that big, warm palm over my right breast. Moisture begins pooling in my panties and I can feel heat moving through my body and centering on all the pleasure receptors in my body. I am preparing to have them blown sky high when he twists my nipple between his fingers. The jolt of pain was so intense I gasp. It's the opening he wanted. He pushes his tongue in my mouth, finding mine and teasing it, drawing it out to play with his. I am helpless to stop it. A woman would have to be dead not to respond to this man's kiss. Our tongues dance and tangle. I can't stop my moan that releases into his mouth. It is a mere vibration, barely a whisper of a sound, but it gives him all the encouragement he needs. I know that by the way his thumb brushes over the erect nipple he had inflicted pain on earlier. My arms circle around his neck as my body pushes in. I need to get closer to him.

I push my fingers into his hair, the texture abrasive and exactly as I imagined. I'm trying to get his mouth closer, even though that is physically impossible. I want to devour him. The kiss turns up another notch, hell another ten notches. His hands move down to my ass cupping it, kneading it and bringing me up his body. His hard cock pushes where I need it most. I'm not sure what would have happened next. I think I might have let him fuck me right there on the porch. I was that ready, that needy, that willing to go there. Until the hoots and hollers from his friends start, my body locks and I pull away, regretfully. I look into his warm dark chocolate eyes, and I have to catch my breath at the beauty.

His fingers bite into my ass. I realize I had pushed my thighs into the side of his like a wanton hussy, but seriously that's what he made me into. I might as well own it. I push against his shoulders and release my legs so he would put me down. Luckily, Bad Nicole was as speechless as me.

Stud watches me and somehow his eyes get darker. Oh they looked good before, but now I melt, and from the sticky wetness between my legs I could honestly say I mean that literally.

I tear my eyes from him and look down at his feet. I feel heat enter my cheeks as the men with him keep ragging at us. He lowers me back to the ground slowly, my heart pounding, beating hard and echoing in my ears.

I step back the minute my feet hit concrete. My fingers come up to my swollen lips, as the world begins to right itself. In the background I can hear the boys making comments. I'm sure it would embarrass me to death, but I can't concentrate. I glance at him and then try to look away, but can't seem to pull my eyes away.

"You should come by the club tonight Twinkie...me and

the boys are just right up the road. We could show you and your girl a real good time,"

I blink. My brain is addled. We? He didn't mean that the way it sounded. Right?

"The club?" I ask confused, trying to focus my thoughts, but that was easier said than done.

"Yeah babe, me and the boys are the Savage MC. Our clubhouse is up the road about fifteen miles. Just take the left by the old barn and follow the road till it veers left…not that hard to find. We're always looking for new Twinkies. You and your girl would fit right in. I'll even make sure you enjoy it personally," he said twirling my hair around his finger.

"I…you…." I stop. I had been looking forward to this man blowing my mind; I just didn't think it would be like this. Damn him telling me this…makes me feel raw inside. It hurts. I can feel embarrassment flooding through me. I hadn't been exposed to that kind of thing, but I did read romance novels. I loved reading Motorcycle Club erotica even. What girl didn't? In my books, I had heard club women referred to as muffler bunnies, mattress monkeys, sweet butts, candy, club toys, and a million other things. They all rounded down to one word. Whore! I had never heard Twinkies, but I could imagine it was one in the same.

"We could make all your hot little wicked fantasies come true baby—every last fucking one, no matter how filthy." He leans down and whispers in my ear.

I pull away from him like his touch burns, and damn it all to hell it did!

After three steps back I look around to see his men in the background behind my car all smiling, leering and joking. I see Dani get away from the guy who had given her a ride.

She walks behind me and Stud with a strange look on her face. She takes the key we had been mailed and opens the door and stands there waiting.

"What makes you think we're looking to be Twinkies?" I ask evenly. I was proud of myself because you couldn't hear the hurt in my voice.

"C'mon babe, no one lights up in a man's arms as quick as you do unless she's hot for it. No shame babe. You want to piss off your rich ass parents? You won't be the first. Just so happens, this time I happen to like the idea of helping you make that goal."

He sounds so cocky and looks so sure of himself. How could I have forgotten my earlier thoughts? Player—total player.

"Sorry to disappoint you Stud, but it hasn't been my life's dream to be a Savage chew toy. Also, I ceased to care what my parents thought of me a couple of years ago, when I pissed them off for the last time. You should run home now, I'm sure you have…Twinkies was it? Twinkies there to take care of all your wicked little fantasies!"

With that I turn around. I thought it was a good line. I am proud of myself. I can tell by Dani's smile she was too. But Stud, won't let it pass. He grabs my hand to pull me back around.

"You can't deny what you were offering Mama. A man can only go by what you put out there."

I take a deep breath. I pull my hand so he gets the message to let me go. He does, but he gives me a look that makes it plain he isn't about to leave until we have this (whatever this was) out.

"First of all, if I remember correctly you started calling

me Twinkie before I offered you jack shit. In fact, I don't believe I have yet to offer you anything Stud. So please stop wasting my time and yours. Run along," I say making a movement with my hand like I was scurrying away a dog. Heck, he is most assuredly a dog.

"Babe, that kiss you sure as hell offered, and you were definitely sending out those vibes earlier."

"Oh my God! I was flirting! Women do that when they think someone standing before them is hot!" He grins, and I swear at that moment I want to slap the shit out of him. How could someone you just met make you feel such a range of emotions?

"And besides that," I continue, before I gave into the urge to kill him, "it was just a damn kiss." I hold up my hand when he starts to argue with me. "It was a fucking kiss, nothing else! I don't even know your name for God sake!"

I turn to the door when his voice stops me, "Dragon."

"What?" I ask, looking over my shoulder to ask.

"My name is Dragon."

"I seriously doubt that, but in either case it doesn't matter as I won't be using it."

"Learn it Mama. Cause trust me, you will be fucking screaming it out and soon."

I ignore him. I mean really, what can you say to that... especially when my body wanted to agree with him. I make it inside the kitchen and slam the door. I lean against it and look at Dani. We stare at each other a minute and then Dani grins.

"So, that was interesting." She deadpans.

I look at her like she had just grown three heads. We hear

the bikes start up outside and then slowly we both start laughing, as I sink to the floor on my ass.

Breaking Dragon's Playlist

Breaking Dragon Final
(open.spotify.com/user/12149197675/playlist/1JWfJFpsf4odID9kg'

Animal
A Real Man Series
Book 15
Jenika Snow

Chapter One

Jessa

I'd known him nearly my whole life.

My father's business associate, the man who put fear in everyone just by looking at them.

Now here he was, sitting at our dining room table, the cigar in his mouth causing a cloud of smoke to fill the small room. He had a square-cut glass of bourbon in front of him, and although my father was speaking to him about the business, Rye watched me.

Rye Jaxon.

Even the sound of his name did something to me. He might've been a business partner with my father, their illegal dealings bringing in loads of money—so much they couldn't even count it—but Rye was the muscle of the two.

He was big, strong, and tall. He was a beast, and all others took in his size and knew to give him a wide girth.

"Jess, sweetheart, I need you to go to your room for a minute."

Although I was nineteen and knew the illegal operations my father and Rye did in order to make money, my father still wanted to protect me. Maybe he was naive in thinking I didn't know what he really did, how he sold drugs and guns, how he did underground business to make a living.

But I knew all of it, heard all the rumors. I'd even seen some of it go down.

I stood but kept my focus on Rye. My father was speaking to him about something, but Rye had his attention right on me.

He lifted his glass and took a long drink of liquor, his gaze locked on mine over the rim of the cup. I felt my body heat rise but suddenly chill at the same time, goose bumps forming along my flesh.

I shouldn't want him—not just because he was my father's business associate, not because he was older than me, but because he was dangerous.

I left and went to my room, shutting the door softly and leaning against it. I felt my nipples harden, pushing against the material of my bra and shirt. I was also wet between my thighs, an instant reaction I had whenever I was around him.

What I needed was to get myself under control because there was no way anything whatsoever was going to happen between us. Even if I threw myself at him, begged him to take my virginity, I knew Rye would never touch me.

But then what was with the looks he gave me? What was with the possessiveness I felt from him as he watched me?

Maybe I'm imagining those looks, that feeling?

No, that wasn't something I could ever imagine.

I knew that I wanted Rye to be my first, wanted to feel his rough, strong hands on my body, holding me down, making me take all of him. This might be in my head, a fantasy of mine, but it was something I wasn't going to let go of.

And Rye was who I wanted, who I'd have even if I had to tell him, show him how ready I was for him.

* * *

Rye

I left Kash's house, my thoughts on Jessa. Hell, I thought about her constantly. She was too good for me, too sweet and innocent, too vulnerable. I was a dirty bastard for desiring her, for imagining the filthy things I wanted to do with her.

She'd been living with her mother until last year, when she'd turned eighteen. But even before she'd lived with Kash permanently, she'd come to visit regularly. I never saw her as anything more than the daughter of my business partner.

But something had changed in the last year. At eighteen Jessa moved in with her father. Her mother had remarried and moved out of state. Jessa hadn't wanted to go with them, and so she stayed here.

I remember that day. She was no longer a child but a woman. She'd just graduated high school, her body all curves. But I told myself not to even think those thoughts of her.

She was far too young for me, nearly two decades younger, to be exact. But it wasn't the age difference so much that bothered me, but the fact that my life was not something I wanted her involved in, even if she was inadvertently because of her father.

Kash also tried to shield her, protect her from the work we did. Maybe it wasn't a living to be proud of, but it was who we were, what we did, and there was no going around it. The best we could do was make sure Jessa was protected.

I entered the bar Kash and I owned, walked past the customers, and headed to my office. The bar was a front, as were the other three businesses we owned: a strip club, a small corner grocery store, and a bar that was on the other side of town. They were to make things go smoothly with the law, to pay our taxes and stay under the radar.

The illegal gun business was where our money came from, and where we got all our connections.

Once my office door was shut, I moved to my desk and sat behind it. I busied myself planning the gun drop for later this week, something to try and get my mind off the one woman who invaded my thoughts constantly.

Kash and I were criminals in every sense of the word. I never tried to downplay it or lie about that fact. But we didn't hurt people unless they tried to do harm to us or the ones under our protection. We didn't terrorize people, didn't bully them or use illicit violence just because. We made money, albeit the illegal way.

We didn't deal guns to kids, didn't try to make an innocent into a criminal. We might not be law-abiding citizens, but when someone needed our help, we were there, no matter who they were, no matter what lifestyle they chose to have.

Kash might have thought Jessa didn't know what we did, how we brought in money. But I was fully aware that she knew how we made a living. Even before she lived with her father, I could see in her eyes the realization and truth of what she knew. She might never have brought it up to us, but she was smart as fuck.

When the drop-off was secure, I disconnected the call, tossed my cell on the table, and leaned back in the chair. I sat there for long seconds just staring at the wall, wanting to go to her, wanting to hold Jessa.

I'd never been a man who thought I could find love, thought I'd ever settle down. But I wanted that with Jessa. I wanted her to be mine in all ways. I wanted to show her that underneath everything I was a good man.

Or maybe I was a delusional bastard in thinking I could have her. Maybe I needed to get my shit straight and come to the realization that Jessa would never be mine. She could do better than me, could find a man who toed the line, who followed the rules.

I growled low, the sound involuntary. Just thinking about her with somebody else, imagining some bastard touching her body, making her feel good, pissed me the fuck off.

No. No one else would have her but me.

Where to find the authors:

Facebook
Newsletter
Pinterest
Twitter
Goodreads
Website

Facebook
Newsletter
Instagram

Twitter
Webpage
Goodreads

CPSIA information can be obtained
at www.ICGtesting.com
Printed in the USA
LVHW081558250119
605132LV00018BA/455/P